Utter Nonsense

Utter Nonsense

A TURN-ON SINCE

A Manuscript From the Future
First Published in 2098

Edited by Clive Burke
Foreword by James Burke

iUniverse, Inc.
New York Lincoln Shanghai

Utter Nonsense
A TURN-ON SINCE

iUniverse books may be ordered through booksellers or by contacting:

iUniverse
2021 Pine Lake Road, Suite 100
Lincoln, NE 68512
www.iuniverse.com
1-800-Authors (1-800-288-4677)

ISBN: 978-0-595-49043-1 (pbk)
ISBN: 978-0-595-60944-4 (ebk)

Printed in the United States of America

"Thaw me dear miss thumb mess sedge"
Ma's shawl Mick low wan

Dead occasions …

Tomb eye broth errant meant half or
hyssop pour tanned in corps regiment, tanks.

Haul sew tomb isle hongs huff a ring
why if baa-baa rough fur hair inn fin nut patients.
Owe, wand knot two fur get
mile idyll peepholes ham, jaw want hilly

Foreword

It is rare indeed for the scholar of future history to be given the opportunity to view and comment on the first edition of a manuscript such as this. As far as we know it is the only one successfully to have transited, undamaged, from a parallel universe (in this case: parallel and future, since it is dated 2098 AD).

Like all archeological fragments, this precious artifact tells us much about the life and times of the inhabitants of that universe. Not only because the timeline at the end of the manuscript describes events very like those in our own history, but because the materials from which the document is made (paper, ink) and the contents (an exhaustive selection of the speeches and writings of that other world) reveal that the inhabitants at least thought and spoke about things common to our own lives. It would indeed be fascinating to have anything that would give us a clearer view of what this universe actually looks like (Do the people have one head? Is black white? Does the sum of the internal angles of a triangle add up to 180? etc.)

Alas, we are left clutching at straws (or, as the writers of the manuscript might say: 'klatch ingots drawers'). Although the texts in the manuscript include comfortably-familiar themes and issues, these matters of consequence could as easily be germane to a universe inhabited as much by monsters or fairies as by people who looked like us. Try as we might, the contents of this manuscript are impenetrably similar to anything found within our own literary canon. It is impossible to discover other abnormalities beyond the abnormality of the texts themselves.

Thanks to the extraordinarily detailed textual analysis by editor (and discoverer of the manuscript) Clive Burke, we have a pretty good idea of the events that may have acted as the trigger for this particular parallel universe. However other scholars have taken issue with the fact Colonel Armstrong's view through his window (immediately on his return from the Ice Age) was extremely limited. All he appears to have been able to see was the welcoming group and their screen.

Opinions, then, are divided as to whether or not the change he saw was indeed limited to language alone. In the absence of further manuscript discoveries, we may never know.

There is one entirely different view of the work, voiced by a lone scholar from the Institute for the Study of Clearer English in Lodz: that the entire manuscript is a hoax and its editor, Burke, a charlatan.

Only you, the reader, can judge.

James Burke

Editor's note

The manuscript (dated 2098 and recovered from the future by means which are at present National Security Top Secret) seems to refer to an event which took place three years before publication. Best guess is that local news reporting might have read as follows:

> *Dateline: 2095 AD. CUS Time and Space Research Laboratory, Chinese-American Bilateral Protectorate of Cuba.*

The first time-traveler in the history of mankind was ready. After decades of development and fine-tuning, the machinery to squirt him back in time was up and running. Armstrong settled back in his capsule, concentrating deeply on the words of Doctor Wells, the Chief Scientific Officer on this project. "Mr General Secretary, sir. I know I don't have to remind you, sir, that this day sees the most important event in the history of science. In a moment, this Hero of the Union will be transported back in time thousands years, to the end of the last Ice Age".

The head of the US Politburo grunted. "Ah so! Cavemen. What can we possibly learn from them?". "Sir, the reason we've chosen the end of the Ice Age is that, with the temperature freezing for so long, we don't expect any problems from bugs and viruses with which modern man would have difficulty. No matter how good our filter systems are, we can never be sure. So, for our first manned venture into the past, we want to play safe".

The GenSec of the United States of the Americas wasn't stupid. "Oh. He won't come back itching then. But maybe he will take something there with him? Won't that be a problem?". He'd been briefed that morning by his Scientific Advisor. Just two or three simple questions he couldn't get wrong.

Never mind that he didn't understand the answers. It was all for the benefit of the media, who were hanging on his every word. The CSO thought for a moment. What could he say about tampering with the past in front of the world's press? "Well sir, we have complete safeguards installed. As soon as Colonel Armstrong steps out of his capsule, he will automatically be cocooned in a force field which will insulate him from actual physical contact with anything".

Seeing the usual bemused look on the Secretary's face, he clarified. "That means he can't create any change to the environment and should remain perfectly safe himself. If he did any damage, the effect down the ages would be totally unpredictable. Imagine, if you can, the result of causing the death of, say, your primitive man. That man could, feasibly, be one of your own ancestors. The outcome would be catastrophic. You would simply cease to exist, sir".

The Secretary's face was inscrutable. "I hope you're not suggesting that I am descended from some stupid primitive, Doctor". The world press dutifully chuckled with the GenSec. His lack of humor was legendary, the required response, mandatory. Wells contained his irritation. "No, Mr Secretary. My little joke. Now, may we proceed with the launch?"

He pressed the button. Almost instantly, Armstrong's view on the outside ports changed. Instead of the inside of the lab, he was looking at a verdant valley and, away in the distance, the edge of a huge ice field. His orders were, the first time, to return immediately, but he couldn't resist the chance to set foot where no man had been before. Neil Armstrong opened the hatch and stepped out, murmuring "That's one small step for a man. One giant leap for mankind", echoing the immortal words of his great-great-grandfather.

There wasn't a sound. The sun shone down on an idyllic scene. Away to the north, evidence of the Ice Age's slow retreat. He cancelled his force field and slid open his filter mask. He knew he shouldn't have done so, but everything was so peaceful, it couldn't do any harm if he just took one sniff of the crystal-clear air.

He felt a bit of a prick. A mosquito was on his cheek, sucking as if there were no tomorrow. This could ruin everything. If the insect picked something up from him, who knew what the consequences might be. There was only one thing to do. With a sharp slap, he snuffed out its life and with it, the danger of leaving an alien virus behind in the mosquito's blood.

Then Armstrong got back into his time capsule and pressed the return button. Thinking "A little thing like that won't shake the earth," he failed to appreciate that the skeeter had been destined to be the morsel that would save the life of a starving humming bird. And that bird would have saved the life of a starving saber-toothed tiger. And, away along the time and food chain, the big cat would one day have been the meal that saved the life of a starving caveman, who was just in the process of learning to make fire, stand up straight and, most important, *communicate.*

The flashing numbers on the digital readout stopped at time-zero. Armstrong looked at his outer ports and breathed a sigh of relief. He had returned safely from the most important journey mankind had ever made. . He cracked the capsule door and began to step out, to tumultuous cheers Across the control center he saw that his colleagues had fired up a huge plasma screen in his welcome. He read it and smiled, though slightly puzzled. All was well with the world. Well, nearly. The screen read …

Eye sage manners writ earned!
WHELK HUM CARNAL KNEEL HAMSTRUNG!
"Thought swans maul steppe ferryman.
Winch high until heap form unkind."

Cosmological note:

When Armstrong snuffed out the tiny life of the mosquito, he performed an act of incalculable significance. You do the same every day. If you go out of the front door and turn right instead of left, you generate a new universe, from then on. As time passes, that universe grows increasingly different from the one in which you turned left. This edited manuscript reveals one small effect of such an event: it presents a selection from the English language of the parallel universe triggered by the mosquito's death.

Editor's note on the manuscript language

Have you ever thought about our confusing mother tongue? And how it came about?
A view aver thaw tub outer can fusing moth art hung? Endow wit game or bout?

At school, we were taught along strict grammatical lines.
It's cool, wee war toddle lungs tricked grim hat tickle lions.

But imagine how it would all have turned out, in a parallel universe,
Bottom edge enow wit wood olive tern doubt, inn up arrow lull you knee verse,

where every kid wrote what the teacher uttered, not what she wrote on a board.
wherever wreck hid row twat that each her rutted, knot watch ear oat tawny bored.

Chaos would surely reign ... but we'd not have to wonder
Case switch early rain ... bat weed knot after wander

why 'sough' is spoken as 'sow' and 'sought' is spoken as 'sort',
wise how wisp oak in a sound sorties poke inners ought,

while 'cough' is spoken as 'cof'. Very confusing for foreigners!
wile coffers poke in a scoff. Ferric on few sing fur four a nurse!

Wouldn't it all be clear and simple? And easy to understand?
Wooden tit tall beak leer rinse impel? Ant teas eat two wonders tanned?

The manuscript presents a wide-ranging set of examples of both the classic and the crass.
Thumb man you scrapped prose sense awe hide rain gins het tough axe samples off bow thick lassie canned thick wrasse.

Read on at your peril … at the very least, this manuscript will banish your insomnia!
Reed doughnut chewer payroll … hat thaw ferrule east, thus man you scrapped twill ban assure rinse some near!

PRIMER TO THE LANGUAGE (off you wheezy once, forest art)

Yell laugh lowers (Yellow Flowers)

A wand hurdle loan layer sack loud,
Thoughtful oats sun hire fails anthills,
Win, allot one size soar rack loud
Arose to goal tend half odd ills,
Bus idle ache, bin ether trays,
Flat herring end and sing end upper ease.

Stew Pit Buoy (Stupid Boy)

Symbol sigh man mat up high mango one two though fare
Set cymbals high meant who dope hymen
Late met hastier where's
Seth hip high mint whose ample sigh mince shawm a furs chirp any,
Sets impulse high manteau though pay manse hurry event hen knee.

Thud Home (The Dome)

Insane ado, duck who black can
Estate leap leisure doomed a Cree,
Wee Ralph, this ache red reaver anther
Hook have earns mesh your list demand

Hound tours unless see-sawed
Why's Fife my all suffer till crowned
Wit waltz sent ours work hurdle drowned.

A wreck no foe beer (Arachnophobia)

Ladle mess muff fits hat owner tough it
Heater knock heard sound whale
Lank aim espied errands at town base cider
Hand fry tinned mess muff fitter weigh.

Haul up-end town (All up and down)

Check on chill, one tap thaw hilt, tough edge up halo, what, her?
Cheque felt town, in brow kiss crow,
None chill camped humble in gaffed her.

Abject cotton, gnome deed rotters foster see wore sable,
Hey win tub head, tum end as said,
Wee finicky rant bran pay poor.

Julie … Ho! Seize her (Julius Caesar)

Terry sat tied, endear fearsome hen,
Wished ache on hat though flawed,
Lids undo four tuna, meted, haul they've high edge after-life
Ass bow-end inch hallow sand enemy series,
Answer chaff fool sear winnow awful oat
On whim mistake thick arrant win hot serfs, sorrel ooze serve ensures.

…. end of primer. Original manuscript text follows.

FEY BALLS & FURRY TAILS

Oaf ox antique row … of hay ball.

Wants the wizard ear lid off hocks, wither glassy redcoat, end hub you tough fool tale. Hay whisk old 'roofers'. Hush harp peers skewed dear thus molests hound; hush sharpen hosed witch debt this molest cent. Her lay wand hay wain thief ox whisper row linger hound, been heath annulled sick amour, hissed rusty knows big hand hoot witch. "Was hat?" roofers head, alter hymns elf "Water one duffel a roamer, as bet earthen or habit. End hits batter thinner hair. As heave in ice earth Ann apple hump fez hunt. Eye wander watered his".

Heap puttees knows toothy grind, hand-drew titter hound, bat that ant icing goader wizened underground. Is snifter gain. Hew wandered wear thus Melanie snows worse combing frumenty live Ted a snows a pie, ends nifty gain. Sodden lay, hick cats high tougher burred, parched eye anther sick amour. At wore sick roe, wand, inert speak, hit whisker rasping sum thin gap at icing; sum thinker assembling as knack; sum thin cattle hooked hasty. Off ox's fey ferret bank quit: crumb Billy ant haste itch, ease!

Deaf ox slicked he slips, sand wandered joss tower craft if ox cud how twitter stew pit burred. Hick hood inch hump pine off tug rabbit. Hick hood ink lime thus sick come whore, big horse head hidden tough clause ash harpers sick hat. On deck who dent event ache toothy errands whooped town nut thick row. Thin thick raft of hocks sadden eye dear. Hill hooked a pat though burred, inch outer doubt "water gorges spurred. Satchel overlay beacons hatch all over lick oat off heathers". Whale, thick roads held dumb herds hutch harming flatter rib off whore, inch his tucker chest tout, inch humped opened how nun dub ranch.

Deaf hocks queued seethe ear fact tit worse halving. Swiss poker gain. "End waters park hill inner rise" his head "Disk row mast beady moss tatter active burden though whirled. Shoe wood bee thick wean offal burred, sieve shake hood single hike inane jell".

Wail! Thicken seated burred cooed enter assists hutch itch ants tubby this enter over tension, in dope penning gets peak, big hand tusk reach. Their racquet! Hit worst hairy ball, end attack owed drowned though would. Thaw while he roofers new jest water axe pecked, hand weighted, thin town felt ditch ease, rye tint wheeze owe pinch haws. Hitch who doughnut, chuck all in wiggle lea.

"Ferret hasty" his headers thick row show to dinner age. "Seams tummy, thatch hood who a verve oyster ewes, spat water petty yew event tub rainy swell!".

Hand thumb horror Liz, Neville isn't tough latter Ray

Ghoul de Luxe endeth repairs … off furry tail.

Wants a porno thyme, dare wear tree pears … feather bare, end mutter bare, end lit all bay be bare. The awl left tug heather, anal idyll how Cindy would. Undecided a would leave dale idyll curly whisk cold "Ghoul de Luxe". Want hay, Ghoul de Luxe set tour madder "Idle actor gopher awoke candor would". Sewer madders head "Whale Isle beacon tent, of yarn hot tool hate combing by comb".

Soak cold dill lox winter rotten Trudy would, answered anally, shove hound ache leering, endear, writing dumb idyll, wore supper idyll idyll louse, worthy tree pears leaved. Bartered repair swear nutty tome. Day wear inner feel doubt cider though would, underwear oven on ice-pick nick. Ghoul de Luxe wrapped under dour ant win dare wizen whore apply, shoe pinned adorned wok tin. Shake aim Tudor kit shone, hand don date able, war tree balls-up a ridge.

Whale, sodden league, goal deal lacks swizzle ladle hung grease, sews shoot rider beg ball, batted west to what. Sushi trite them idylls iced ball, batted west took hold. Den chit rider let all ball, ended wears joust trite, associate a tall hop. Thin shoe end hops tear, sent fountain dab head rheum tree bets, be long in tooth or threw beers.

Shoes abets leap pea, sushi troy do pig bet, batted west toward. Tense shut ride term idylls iced bet, butt hat whist whose off tense shoot writer ladle pedant, hat worse chest riot. Sew Ghoul de Luxe fail fosters leap.

Sunday tree bursar hive dome, meant wanton toothache itching. "On toes bean neaten may purr edge" set thaw feather bare. "Aunt hose span heating may poor age" set thaw mutter bare. "Into spin heat in may paw ridge" set thaw bay peep errand "the feet in a tall hop".

Tendered repairs wind-up stares, tug oat tub pedant twinned hay wain tinder durum, feather bare sad "Hose pants leaping enemy pedant" mutter bare sad "Into spins leaping him wipe head" hand bay peep hearsay "Dent Hugh's bin slip in enema pedant shoes to linnet".

Jaws ten, Ghoul de Luxe walk cup, sorter tree pears tearing doughnut hair, chum tout herb head, rash doubter dick caught age, Trudy would, beck term hum he … undo haul lift a pulley heave a rafter.

Let all read *(passed hence)* Dryden nude.

Wants serpent thyme, dare wassail idyll curlew lift wither muttering her caddie John decide over dance would. Shoes scold let all read Dryden nude.

Wendy, harm udders head "Let all read Dryden nude, a win shooter runway a bass skitter feud tug random madder's. Shoes knot fairy wail sushi Sinbad, sauté curse hum goody stewer coat agenda otters cider Defoe rest."

Sheep putter Ed Dryden new don, aunt hooked he Basque ate frame more mud errand when tooth agate. "Noun owe dodder ling" colder mutter "Ghost rate toothy cot edge, jest stain door par thin dunce peaked toast rangers"

Let all read Dryden nude ripple eyed "Hawkeye, aisle beak earful" land aft shoe ain't.

Shoe whence keeping in topping, Trudy for rest, stain under bath, jostle liquor Madrid tolled hair. Sadden leaf rum our hound hub bus shout champ tab Ichabod Wilf. "Hallow let all curl "Sid though Wilf "Underwear hair Hugo wing wither bee keeper feud?"

"Tomb high ground matter's cut hedge. Shoes second embed ant time coin tomb ache curse sums up her" let all read Dryden newt's head.

"Water could ladle curlew war" set thew elf "Oft chew Goa thin, an seethe thud dear lay day."

Let all read Dryden hoot rotted oaf, fanned thew Wilf set whims elf "Hoe, white ink isle goat who peg grunt madder recall". Dennis nicked aft threw thaw would.

Chortle leak aim toe ground madder's coat agent apt under dour. "Hugh's knack anon thud whore?" cold grunt madder. "Hits meager random adder" thaw Wilf's head "Hive braw chews ham feud". Soothe holed grunt madders head "Left thole hatch hand wore kin".

Puerile grainy cued dense heave hairy whale, ant's head "Hollows, wheat tart, tits kinder view Turcoman seer owl ground madder … sew otter weaving furred inner?"

Thaw elf sad "Dwell, isle bee halving you've hard inner" randy champed under pedant hate heron won beg Alp. Denny gotten tube head, poult thick avers upend weighted.

Sioux knoll hunk aim let all read Dryden nude. Shoot apt anther do randy wall fin ovary hive ice head "Due asset?" anthill idyll curl ripple eyed "Hit slit ill read Dryden nude, camped a visa chew, Grenadier"

Endue elf's head "Live tool hatch end woken, muddier" insole, atoll read Dryden nude upended whore, end wok tin.

"Ogre end mutter, wet bag here shove cot" settle let all read Dryden nude. "Older butter two weary a wit, muddier" sad though elf.

"End wart bag ice shag hot" Sid let all read Dryden nude. "A lob batter toss sea ewe wit, muddier" sat thew Alf.

"Endow hot begat heath yew halve" saddle let all read ride a nude. "Alter battered wheat chewy thumb, muddier" set thaw elf, thin edge hump tout tufty pedant thence wallowed let all read ride a nude hole.

Jest enough rend lay witch hopper, worst riding pasty coat edge, interred old dark emotion. Hedge hump tint truth adore, rinse sore thaw beg bard Wilf, justice eats wallow delay doll curl hole. Soda witch up pearl if teddy's pig hack sand gift though alpha pig thumb, panic ill dims toned head.

Olive is sodden, knee aired "Hell pass! Hail purse!" combing frame mince hide though elf, soothe once winger fish choppy wreak hut thaw Wilf owe pennant let all read Dryden nude, end hair ground madder, wearable touch hump pout.

Eat hook let all read Dryden nude omen day olive dapple hay off our rafter.

Check under bin stoke … off hairy tail.

Along lung dime ego, inner faro hay can tree, lifters maul buoy culled "Check", "Cheque", whores humped I'm "Shack". Know, Check lift widow smother, weed out Wanky, e'en arouse neural larch cars hole.

Wendy, cheque worsen dig hard on, win weed out Wanky cull doubt a whim "Check mid-ear, wear how tough hood, on weave gnome Mormon hay, sew, saddle hay, ewe laughter ticker kow-tow marquee tense hell lit.

Check when toothy buyer, ran tide thick out oar opened, sat after thin hereby fill age. Asset rotted a long width hick how, Check herd a smother, culling gaff trim "Yule seat hook how byres. A fugue owe tooth earth inn wan, ream ember, heel trite touch heat ewe. Bees your heed assent polder willow furrier ice".

"Dawned war a yob outer thin, guile beak earful, madders" head Check, Andy's het toff wither kow-tow mark it. Check smothers mild, inset two wars elf "Shackle dowel rite, ease ache hood buoy".

Bind buy, her itched thaw fill itch, handmaiden off her tooth half hat byre, hose head "Dime nut bind hood hay, jests Helen" thin Cheque when toothy udder Byron set whim "Whale ewe by the scow, fort end hollers?" twitchy hand sword "Knob, hut isle off for ewer beg arm edge ache bins … been switch wool knot aver rune now't. Sawyer madder want knead moany fur feud, aver hog gain, hype raw miss. Welsh hack wasp leased. "Moth aural beer eel yappy" heath ought, under a gnome toot Ella. Bat madder whiz rill yap set. "Owe Cheque" shoe ailed "the spins sore chest ordain airy bins! Know-all weaken dew whisk hook demand heat thumb".

Off towards, Shack worse fairy sadden twenty rounder corn her, toss it tinder guard hen. Head capped won been, soothe Bess sting wood bee, heath ought, who plan tit. Atom mite groan tool hots off bins, sand may kiss mad whore a pea. Aft awards, Check winter pedant fellows leap, hand reamed add ream, weary beak aimer itch prints.

Hurly thaw neck stay, wench hack whoa cup, peel hooked outer do win dough wand, therein thug hard on, his sorer bins talk, witch when tap an open till hick cue dense ether tap. Check one trashing oats hide, dance tart head hook lie map. "Beak hair filch hack" show Teddy smother "Done archers elf". Check ant sword "Isle bay oak hay" hand hop peak limed.

Hick lime den teak limed, on Tillie worse sofa wrapped, attic hood sea firm isles … rite hovered a cut edge, dark asshole, fill edge ant feels bay yawned. Sonic aim toothache loud, sand whinny gut threw thumb, heel hooked a croissant sore rack asshole, end up ridge.

Fool off Curia City, cheque cryptic cross dub ridge. Whinny ridged thud whore, cheque sore hit wore soap pennant wanton toothy haul. Heap eared are hound, dense sore aster ranges height. This tears, thatch hairs, that able, a very abject wizen hoar mouse.

Heat tipped hoed threw adore, random omen till lay turf, hound dumps elfin thick itch hen. Jester sickened lay terrier duck rash, in third whore flue up in. Their, sicks thyme sash Hugh jazzy whores, stewed hen hug ledge high ant. Thatch eye hence tumbled overt tooth at hay ball, satin itch errand when tussle heap. Hew whiz ferried rank, witches way heed hidden siege hack.

Check apt ferric whiten, lay tour, to kill hooker hound, dense hawthorn estover run thought able, lands hitting gone knitwear sag ooze. Thug ooze adjust lady's hollered goal den Hague, haul shy knee hand knew.

Check diss sided toast heel thug ooze antique a tome, tomb makers smother itch end a pee. Swig atoll dove thug who sander runny whey, acre rust dub ridge, toothy bints talk. Allot wants, thug ooze big hand toy hell "Hell puss, mast hair! All pass muster! Wick hop, weigh cop! Massed amass stir! A stake enemy aweigh!" Sad only, chequered "Fee Fife hoof home, eyes male double lad oven ingle ash moan. Bee heal hive, orb bee hid head, Elgar rind hiss boons, tum ache hum highbred". A twist thatch high ant, comb enough trim!

"Hose" quelled check "High mast gaiter weigh" ankle limed hound a bins talker squiggly espouse able. Wen egg hot toothy bought ham, hay wain tint other cut agent cotton knacks, andiron toothy bins token chapped tit town. Thatch high ant fail oaf, phantom omen dilator, felt toothy grind, end dyed. Checked hook thug whose enter thick coat edge, inch odor smother thug holding ooze, sand-shoe toll dimwit ache lever sunny wars … sandy haul lift a pulley off a rafter.

Tree bully coat scruff … off able.

"A noble laugh, enable huff, thaw lift tree bully coat scruff, ladle bully go, tomb idyll bully go, tag rate beg bully go tug ruff"

Thought south as hung owes snow heiress defer retail …

One slung dime ergo sum coats lift enough heeled buyers trim.

Thaw wore off Emily off coats culled "Ballet coats, grrr, huff!".

Wendy, though ladle coats head twist who burr others, "Thug wrasse series knee ear lea elfin itched, battle hook covered hair, hits longhand fairy grin. Soil chest rotter cross, sand heater bitterns seer fit stay stay."

Andover hew ant, 'treat rot, treat rot', hover though rick a tube ridge.

A lover's sad hen, rite infer ant have hymn, map eared hen gnaw ribald wharf, wither norm must heath, hand on arm musk laws. Hit wizard red fault roll land hits hang:

"Eye mat roll, fold a roll,
Eye mat roll, fold a roll,
Eye mat roll, fold a Roland aisle itch shoe furs upper!"

Though ladle go 'twas fairies cared, bat thawed ferric wiggly, hands head "A fuel atom ego, wand weight ermine it, Yukon neat mime idyll sighs broth hair, easel hot meteor thin eye yam".

Soothe hat roulette impasse, sandy when 'treat rot, treat rot' hover ant tooth off heeled, worth hag ring wrasse crew.

Shored hilly, thumb idyll bully go tug ruff fell tongue gray hand thaw tit wood beer g'day dear tug hoe owe veer, sew a fee when 'treat rot, treat rot', hover thaw rick a tube ridge.

Awl over sadden, that rolls prang outer Timon's hang:

"High mutter hole, folder hole,
High mutter hole, folder hole,
High mutter hole, folder hole, land eyelet chew force up her!"

Thumb idylls iced go 'twas fairies cared, bat all sew thawed ferric wiggly, hands head "A fuel atom ego, wand weight ermine it, Yukon neat migrate beg broth hair, ease heave van meteor thin eye ham".

Soothe hat roulette impasse, sandy when 'treat rot, treat rot' hover in tooth off heeled, worth hag ring wrasse crew, end a slit hole broth hair wore seating hit.

Necks, talon game crate bag belly coat graph, wither sin whore mouse fee tendon harm muss said, 'Thumb, path thumb, path thumb, path thumb pa', hover thaw rick a tube ridge.

Ouch hump toot roll, lands hang:

"Arm hatter awl, falter all,
Arm hatter awl, falter all,
Arm hatter awl, falter all, in toil a view verse hopper!"

Bat crate bag belly coat graph, worst all errand strung girth hand it roll, Andy buttered dim sew ward, ditty flue rite a pinned he hair on lend head under moo, nanny's tilth hair, tooth hissed hay … sow, wane nuts awful munificent higher lick leer, enough Yule hook-up, Yukon seem Lou king downer chew!

End dumb aural hiss, "aboard underhand, spatter thin twin-tub hush".

Racks tore hitches … of hair writ ale.

Though one's war sick hurl, cold Cindy Roller. Shoes fairy prat tea. Shoes fair yard wore kin. Bat chews ferry a nappy. Use sea, Cindy Roller lift weather whack heads tape mutter, hood too weed dynasty, haggle lead otters. Cindy Roller secrete lick all dumber rug lease his terse, ease push alley, winch sheet hawked turf rend, batons. Batons swore serf Arthur serf intend, heed dead-end lie curses terse, seethe air.

Thug leases terse work cold "Grease elder Andorra". The wharf fairies hell fish, shunned maid baton, sand Cindy Roller, dew olive thaw hearken thaw manner rouse, worthy lift. Want hay, thwack heads tape mutter rash tinder thaw rheum, mince head "Lesson two mead otters. One eye worse sat mark hat, arroyo lair old denounced her grate ballot twitch though kinks Hun, thaw prints, Welch whose hub ride". "Heel sole act thaw must booty vulgar lend dope Alice, sew weave tomb aches hurt tenure hatch Abbess, Tandy mite shoes wan or view. Whale beer itch four reverend, wheel knave a rafter toy lever or gain". Wealth hat worsen nod think terse hay, big horse thin heifer toy led den away.

Purse Cindy Roller cut fairy axe height hid, dunce head tour whack heads tape mutter, "Battered owned oven iced rest aware, own Leith ease racks". Whore whack heads tape mutter cake hole dance hoed hid thought who waggle assist hearse. This head "Dough want beast hoop head, curl, yearn hot combing. Yule laughter hell puss gate red-eye, hand off towards Yukon's crab thick hitch in," hand aweigh though ant.

"Owe batons" swept Cindy Roller, "High wood soul hike tug hoe toothy bawl. Eyed dunce oppose thaw prints wooed thank aim prat tea, batted wood burial in ice, two locket holder prat hick loathes. Battle knots he thumb, big horse, hive gutter a main it tome. A snot fare!".

But tense hand sword "Notes hurt anally knot fares, hinders. Bat aisle gay viewer rand, end weakens hit touts Haydn ear thumb you sick. Thin Yukon prat end, thought chew rat thud hence, sand chew want bee some is arable". "Batons, sure are heel fray end Tommy" set Cindy Roller.… Thud Dave doughball are hived, dandy hug lease his terse, whereat therm host horror ball. "Cindy Roller, brash may air"; "Cindy relic lean mesh ooze"; "Cindy Roller, I earn mike loathes".

Cindy Roller whisk lad Wendy haul go tint toothy car rage, in twenty way tooth had ants. Bats hinder Ella wassail idyll bits had, inch header ladle tier. Thought ear rand own arch he candor hop toff, straighten two this hinders, swear hit maid all lit up huff fist team.

Whale, this team crew went crew, anthill at whizzes bickers hinder Ella. Haul over sadden, thick loud oaf's team beak aimer ferry, witty why trestle spar clay, under wan dinner rand. "Beano tough raid, Cindy Roller, rye menu gnaw arm" sad though furry. "Whore ewe?" subbed Cindy Roller "Rand wire year?". "Lay tit bean own, the time yore furry goad mutter, Cindy Roller, runt hive comb tug heave view yard heiress twitch. Water ewe wash foremost hinder whirled, ear?" Wall, Cindy Roller dead-end knead tooth inker bout tit fur fairy minimum ants, traitor weigh shoes head "High wood loft ago toothy bawl, land ants wither prints. Buttock ant, hive knock loathes, endive knock carry jaw whore says.".

"Whale" chuck holder ferric odd mutter, "Use shell goat toothy bawl" thence shoes head tube Batons "Runny whey, endeavor surge four to itemize, up hum kin, entail Liz hard", hand Batons window weigh, tool hook fourth thumb.

Necks, though ferry goad mutters head "Noose under Ella, eye won't shoot hook low sure ice, hunt horn or hound, toot urns." Cindy Roller dead witch heed bent holed. Winch shed fin itched, whore haggard rest horned in tour itch ledge you welled, lover leg own, enter roll choose big game upper off crease tolls leapers, covert tin dime hands, switch feet header lie keg love".

Butt in speared outer know wherewithal love thaw height my sander pump keen, entail Izzard. Wither waiver forewarned, though furry goad muttered earned thumb ice unto up periphery vines tall ions, anthem a sieve pump keen to wore car edge, ant thaw Liz Arden dwarf hoot manning grinning cold.

Thence shoes head "Aweigh ago, Cindy Roller, Yule hooker hilly booty fall, handy prints wealth ink soar swell. Butter most wore new. Mime eject earns so fat midden height. Some aches your tool heave python knight send, big horse a tall chain jester hag sand my son thaw lest row come hid knight. No waft tooth had ants".

Batons waif tench out head "Huff average holly thyme" Mandy weigh want thick courage. Bind buy, there hive data beg in trance, worth huff hoot monsoon owe pinned thud whore, furs Cindy Roller, ranch he when tin. Shoes lowly wok tin toothy bawl rheum.

Thud hence flour worse fuller peep-hole, luff lea wee men ant hands amen, bitten owners Ann Summers thaw prints. Sad only, ever a buddy's whore Cindy Roller, anther hole plays big game quite tense till. "Whiz the skirl" ever a once head "Shim host beer heel Prince Esther bead rests whore itch lay". Stray to whey, prints chair mingle hooked hat Cindy Roll errand a mediate lea sheaf felon luff.

Though prints aster foray varied ants, anti-felon laugh wither two. Cindy Roller wizened jawing gaurs elf's home hutch, shed hidden denote as thought thyme, thence shared thick locks trike midden height. "Oak" ride Cindy Roller, toothy hung prints, "Eye after gown how", wonder hushed touted up Alice.

Ass thick locks truck though lost row cough two elves, Cindy relate ripped hand lustrous lip hair, patchy cape droning, big horse, hurl over leg own western in Tuaregs. Shower annulled away owe monsoon, though waggle lease cyst hearse wok tin, big herring hand are queuing.

Cindy Roller's head "Ditch who average holly thyme, hat thud hands?" Though waggle lease cyst hearse mooned "Know weed hid dent! Thaws serve hairy ordain Harry loo king garland, though prints staid wither olive thin height ant, weak hood ant git knee rum. Justice swell you'd hid dent comb inure hags, cosh Hugh dove bin rely outer plaice."

Cindy Roller adder quite chuck a lance mile, batted whizzes had won, big horse, chic hood rim amber though prints sold tinker inners harms, sand ants sing wither, rand new show wooden averse sea hymn or gain. "Doughnut beam miss arable" wasp haired baton slate her "Attlee stewed hands twit hymn, handy felon laugh witch who."

Know, backer dope Alice, sever hay won worse Russian go round, haul inner pan ache. "Owed dandy knees" heady prints twist chants cellar "Shoe horse thumb host lover lick curl hive averse e'en. Wally averse sea hairy gain?"

Dandy knees head "Doughnut a spare, you rye ness. Assure anyway, shed raptors leper. No, wit mast bell hung toes ham won, sew wall weave gutter dues finder, input a tone, endophyte feet sit mast bay hair."

"Dandy niche shoe up reclamation, the tombs owe aver these leper shod feet, dab prints solemn merry" whore dared though prints "Goon how, base hurt tenure a tern wither curl." Dandy kneed rovers hoarse tooth haul emits, bat fount gnaw buddy two feet this leper. Finely hick aim toothy man arouse, swear Cindy Roller lift wither whack heads tape mutter, unto waggly cyst hearse.

Thaw whiz crate hacks height mint, tinder rouse. Grease elder Andorra rash tub ouch, outing hat Cindy Roll a target there pest tresses sand brash though rare. Purse hinder Ella wore swore now't Wendy wharf in ashed.

The yawl wend ounce stares, sand prison Ted thumbs elves stew dandy knee. "Eye ham forced" crumbled Grease elder. "Gnome he forced" wined whore a rand gay verse his terrors lap. Has though wharf heighten, dandy knee no test Cindy Roll asset ingot debark after humans head "Wallow isle yew tour ark queuing, thistle aid deem height a swelter eye"

"Owed haunt beer a dick you louse!" cuckold thaw haggle assist hearse. "Shoe wasp pack irk hooking whores up her". Dandy knees head "Though prints sword heard, the tall curls swill tripe hooting thistle hippie Ron" ant hip pat thug lass leper two Cindy Roll as futon, Assisi ass sonny think, kits lipped awn, hand fat-head lie car clove.

Chaste hat thought mow meant, thaw furry goad mutter ape-eared, ant hutched Cindy Roller's racks wither Madge ache one, dander mediate lit earned thaw racks enter aye booty fooled wrasse. Cindy Roller wizen stint liter rants farmed, tinder thaw wander foal booty, witch prints chore mink head foal Lenin laugh wit. Thence shoe wore stake into dope Alice, wishy-washy own interred ditch appellant Mary Tudor prints.

Patchy dead-end for gaiter award off rends. Shoe maid but answer night, hair feather are oil dew candor whack heads tape mud errand hug lease his terse, swear pat two war candy kitsch hen, wear this till walk two the stay … anther print, sand Cindy Roller, lift a pulley off a rafter.

Hands hauling grit all … off ferry tail.

Though wants lifter pour would cut her, randy stew chill drain. The wore cold "hands hauling grit all". Thatch ill drain smothered hide win the war fairy lit land there farther add mar raider gain. Thirst tape madder worse saw wick head purse seine, hoot hold thumb awful though thyme, munch he'd hid dent ache air off the mat tall.

Thaw would cut her add fairy lit all moony four feud, sew the yawl ware hung grim owe stuff thaw thyme. Thin won height, hands hauling grit all whirl lion gall musters leap, Wendy herd thirst tape mutter wisp hair tooth hair farther "Weave tomb aches hums Sirius dizzy shuns. Weave in off hood fur tube hat knot four fore. Witch mean swim most gaiter hid of hands hauling grit all."

Grit hulk ride, winch herders tape madder disk ripe house shoe wit ache ditch ill drained deepen toothy far wrist, handle heave thumbed hood high. Hands held hid ant lettuce hissed torque right tomb hutch. Hip puttees harm surround heron's head "Dunk rile idylls hissed her, aisle hook off tore hew. Isle finder weight hug gaiters pack".

Thin axed hay, hands hauling grit all wart ache in furry weigh. "You're a main ear, anthill wick hum tug hitch who" set thick gruel's tape madder, thence shoe winter whey. Sue knit whist harkened itch ill drain ware holly loan. Grit all size swept bit or tiers, bat hands held rider ice sands head "Drier rice slid holes hiss tear. Luck, winch he wasp ringing a seer, high whist rapping ladles tones underground, forest hoof hollow beck" hunch your on huff, stray chin or wane tethered is stance, all liners tones wish hoeing thumb thawed erection toot ache.

Coal don't hired, hands hauling grit all are hive dome, anther farther wasp lease toes heath hem, big horse hidden ever rug reed withers tape madder. Butch he worse sea crate lead as appointed. Soothe a neck stay, Wendy would cut her whist tillers leap, shoot hook thumb toothy furry stag hen. Hands held hidden half thought I'm tough hinds tones, butt hooks ham bred ant, ass see winter long, hid rapped more cells tough hollow, Wendy wore a loan.

Bat win thatch ill drain trite hoof hind thick rums, awful lock off pitch in sad heat on thumb. Grit hulk ride "Whirl assed, wattle wit who?" Herb wrath ergot two thug round, hand wisp haired "Weal goat tussle heap, panned wane nets mourning, whale hook far away beck". Soothe allayed own in twenty's leap".

Hole though lit hulk reach hearse Cindy for rest tuck pit yon thumb, handle aid rile eaves hover thumb, toss top thumb gate ink hold. Thin axed mourning, hands hauling grit alchemy way curly. Though chilled wrench hose won weigh, in thin thatch hose odd if front whey, bat thick hood dent seethe hat rack.

Bat sodden lathe hay sorrel idyll louse, maid off gin job red, wither hoof a phonic hake, in twin doze off barrel lay shook her. Big horse thought who chill drain worst halving, this tart head tub rake cough peace says sand gabble thumbed town. Oliver's sad hen, Theodore rope hand, handout camel idyll hold aim, wither wok hence tick, hand-up pigs mile.

"Whelk ham, lid ill once" chic hackled "Comb ear, mid-ears. High murk hind hole laid he. Aisle coo queues ham feud". Shoes mild sewn icily, thatch ill drains topped Bianca frayed, din one tin.

Chic hooked thimble otter reel ladle light full feudal thinks thatch ill drain ever adder tome. Thence, shut hacked thumb opener come for table, worm, bad, worthy winter rite toes leaper gain.

One hand's hauling grit hell work captain axed hay, thin ice hold aim mad beak hum ovary fry tannin which. Though which tuck hands hell in putty meanest wrong Cajun luck tit. Shoe maid grit all lie tough hire, thence chef horsed hurt took hooker broth heron a norm mussed inner. "Isle may queue strung on fatten thin eye leech hoof hard inner. Isle hike me tea buoys".

Endeavor red hay, shoe wood putter rand threw thick agent pin chancel reel a yard, tough hind off heed groan. Bat hand sell whist took lever. Hick hood seethe hatch heeded dents heave hairy whale, Zoë hell doubt on holed boa nun twin shoe felt hit, shed a side hid tea whist till tooth in.

Thin wand hay, shed a sided two weight null hunger rants head tug grit haul "Red-eye urn hot, tits thyme tweet. Whelk hook comes traitor weigh. Owe pen thaw a vendor, ankle lime mint toothy haven't whose he off hit sot". Grit hauls head "Eye dunce he wet eye after dew" sew thaw itch clam burden toothy haven't two letters he though waiter due wit.

Alert wants, grit hauls lambed thud whore, anther which worst rapped fur river endeavor. Sue, Nan sell worse outer thick age, hinge humping forge ahoy.

Thatch ill drain explode thick hot agenda wait that hop, founder rheum fuller boxers handbags, witch worst huffed fuller golden chew wills. Soothe haze tough Tasmania's thick hood in tooth harp hock hits.

Neck stance hauling grit all when tout, thin-set oft defined away beck, toothy ladle louse worth hair farther worse sway tin fourth hem. Sodden lathe ache aimed tour aging toe rent, ink hood anchor russet. "No wheel knave horsy feathery gain" thick ride. Hoe lover sadden, these oars wan, witches head "Chum pantomime host rusty beckon isle tick cue toothy udders hide".

Ferric wick lathe, each ill drench hump don't who this once beckoned worse sooner cross. "Think youth and queue" thick ride tooth hearse won. Anthem maid there weigh foreword, threw thought recent pushes. Thin thick aimer cross hat rail witch seamed family errand, a weigh in did his stance, this haw the roam, wither far theirs hitting, lieu kings had in four lawn.

Whinny sew thumb, third alighted farther rugged the mints head "Yard red false tape mutters gunner wafer river, sewn how, weaken haul lift tug gather a pulley, over rafter". Soothe aid hid.

Thought taught us, sandy hair … owe fey ball.

Deepen thick contrail lifter taught us handy hair. Thaw hair wash your rim mast bedeck wicker stair anther hole whirled. Heath ought the teak hood dental ooze sinner ace, big horse heed thirst wrong guess till eggs. Hidden ever a fuse ditch all hinge, hand in ever law stir ace. Ore … knot anthill thawed hay wain haematemesis taught us, whose head two whim "Eye bitch home eye has band wood be chew inner ace". Wealthy airburst tout chuck a ling, hat this height off thought taught us, whose low liquor hauled passed.

"Hymn foster thin eye? Impasse sable!" his head, dent thin hymn aid abet wither tart houses misses. There range mints work wick lay maiden thin axed hay, althaea knee mills camel long, terse heath erase. "Fife author eat who won" count head thud hog, hook aim two add Judy Kate, ant inner flesh, missed a hair streak to weigh, in dizzy peered in tooth hid his stance.

The never a bud itch ear dismiss tart taut is low lease tumble doff. Furs tea sloe league hot tweeze fore feat. Next heap hoot won futon frond off Theo thereon doff heat rotted, fairies lowly. A very bodice head "Paw taught us, his knot gut itch ants, big horse ceased whose low". Bat toffee when ten away.

Mean wild ashen go whale hiker runny wait rain, hearse head tombs elf "Taut asses smile saw haze sew wives humped I'm fur raise leap". Heiress teddy said honor hock, ankle hosed assize, sin felon toured heaps leap. Along tie impasse dander long gambled missed hare taught us. His head knotty whirred, in can't in nude honors sway, kerf a lance teddy. Sever all ours past tan this son big enters ink. Messed her hair wore cup, imp eared her hound, encode ant seat ought us. "Hymn mast beast hillock croissant thaw farce hide off though woul" messed her hairs head, "Plan tee off thyme farm meter wind erase" handy weight toothy fin a shin lie neat rotted.

Batters sick Eamon's eye tufty lion, Esau thumb oast humble leave a bills height. Upper ready vim, thought taught us whist aching thistle low, fine all paste twin door ace, hand haul thick row twitch ear-ring. Justice missed a hairy rived, pan tin handshake in, they had Judy Kate whores head "Eyed éclair…. mis-start taught us…. THOUGH INNER!". Anther taut ass quite lissome mild unsaid "High mite bees low, batik heap in mine dug hole".

End dumb aural hiss teddy ants low all weighs wince.

Thaw line in thumb house … if able.

Deepened age hung gulf arrow whale lift termite eel line. Though line whist wrong empower foal end, win ear oared, thug round shuck, hand holler thumb hankies sand cocky chews, ranch hatter ring, too wide a waif rum hymn.

Haul off thick reaches Cindy jangle wary fray door vim, hank hauled hymn 'thick keen gather jangle'. A special leaf freighter vim, wassail lid dulled a fence lissome house. Thumb housemaids sore ten thatch heed hidden tallow hearse elf took hum tune ear toothy lining Kay's heat rod honor, hence quash tureen tooth thug round. Thought wood beaver reap pane foal.

Wendy, asking lined roused tundra treat taken he's snap, thumb house whisk cattle linger bout, luck infer cedes tweet. Shame aid or weigh uppers mall ill … horse owe sheath ought. Buttoned Ruth, shoe whisk liming a cross though line stale. Butter surf feat rant hick linking line, Hugh wore cup, wither miter whore. Dip ore ladle mow stropped two thug round, hand inner flesh, line add egg rate poor honor tale.

"Witty youth ink yore apt who" ear humbled "Juno Hugh eye yam?". Wealthy lit hulk reach horsehide. "A wide who, hide who, yore matches stay. Opal ease pare mile eye fend, want hay, high mighty vendue this aim four yew". Wendy line herd thumb house as king firm heresy, heath rue backer said, handle aft. "Eyed reel alike toss heath hat." hiss head "Batch shoe maid meal half, soil etch ago." Heal if teddy's poor, rant thumb house cut hole to weigh, threw thug ring wrasse.

Summit high mill ate her, allot off fun terse wok tin tooth edge angle, handle late raps fourth Ian a mills. They'll aid Annette ache roster mane jangle rowed dandelion, low ping all long, grants trait in twit. Sodden lethal line whist angle dent rapped internet. Anther moor hissed rug old, thumb moray whist rapped.

Hill aid beckoned his mill lick ride, four hoof eared the tea wooden ever risk ape. Furrow hay, thumb house hair disc reams, sank wiggly rant who hiss hide. "Note smite urn two whelp ewe" shoe sedans traitor waist, tart head tune awe there open, denote timer tall, shed maiden off spays, towel howl line took raw lout. "Hi-ho yum highlife" hiss head "Weal beef rends four river endeavor".

Thumb aural: Won could earned as surfs on other.

All add in anthem edgy clamp … ovary tail.

Heresy fairest range store hay, a bout tall hazy buoy culled "All add in". Hiss farther add hide men hay ears sago, wand hiss paw muttered a spared, furry whisk hood fern no thin. Shoe hurried the tea wood-ant avert ache edge hob, butts penned awl hissed hazel hazing or hound, enduing up salute lean know thing.

Want hay, all add in worse hitting, wand herring watered who wither stay, one assed ranger up roach dim, mince head "Assure neigh mall add in?" twitch all add dins heady wars. "Wall-eye ham yore un-cool, ewer feather's broth hair, endive beanie waif harmony ears," axe planed thirst ranger. "Eye hammer itch march ant. Eye may duff or tune, in dimes soap lease tough fine dew. Know, wide lie cute hoot ache edge hob wittier un-cool. Aisle may cure itch hand sucks as fool".

Winch he herd thin ooze, all add in smother wisp leased. Butch heed hidden trek hog nice thought thumb march ant wizen notice anklet tall, butter skimming wheeze heard. Holy wassail hooking four whizzer nuns aspect ink boyhood beast hoop hidden after dewy ferried if a cult ask forum.

Thin axed hay, thaw his hard lead all add in interval ease sand mount tins. Justice Saladin's pearl eggs wary bow two claps sunder rim, thaw is harden ounce tool add in "Wear earmuff fain fell low" wand, sodden late tool add in supper rise, heath ruse hamster ranged us ton thug round, end matter dispel.

Stray to weigh, thug round wish aching. Tool add in sum maze meant, as tones lab up eared, end thaw wheeze hard tip titters hide, tour a feeler fly tough stares, dizzy peering threw thud hark onus billow. Thaw was hard ragdoll add in toothy agents head "Your tug hoe-down this tears, handle hook four hay guard in. Eye can tent earthy guard on, big horse hive adder cur sleighed, witch miens isle dyer fie puttee futons hide. Yule fine dumb edgy clamp hinder guard on. A fughetta thumb edgy clamp, pink comb beck hair-oil may cure itch, be on chewer wilder streams".

All add end ease end dead this tones tearaway, button hot beef whore hip hut honoring, witch thumb mannered tolled hymn wood she'll dim again stall leave ill. Hick aim tooth hug hard on, ants tumbled ache russet wreak hovered inn nest range saw tough root. All add-ins toughed allot off root tint who wisp hock it, thence potted ill lampoon at able.

Heat hook though lampoon clam bird back-up this tears. Thumb manse head "An debt up-end eyelet shoes cape", bat all add in dead ant rust hymn, manse head "Fur stew after Andover mire award". Thumb mannered knot axe pecked head two ears hutch Harry's ponce, sand big game fairy whiled. "Full ash buoy" his creamed, hand dish hut this lab, handful led fur oft tool hand along wear whey. Puerile add in whistle own in fair risk haired. Hear rubbed is sands tug heather, handy spared. Buy missed ache, hear robbed thaw wring end, olive is sodden, edgy knee up peered, dumbbell owed "Eye ham though gene knee off thaw wring, end your mime aster. Water yew ash four?". All add in waist head knot ham omen tense head "Eye wan tug hoe beck tummy madder" rants traitor weigh, fount hymns elf a tome.

He's madder whist alighted. Thin all add in shod dearth thumb edgy clamp on, winch he sore writ, cherub tit, bee corset whisk rhyme me. Want so gain, off hears hum gene knee up eared, unsaid "Eye ham though gene knee off thumb edgy clamp, on your mime aster. Water yew ash four?". Whale strait a weigh, a lad in order define fees tenor mediate lissome feud a peer, don pressure scold impel eights.

Thin all add honcho disc election off root tour smother, hose head "Thesis hag rate four tune inch who will, Saladin. There itchy stew ills hive scene. Yew mast tide thumb a weigh, fair essay flea." Sew they'll hocked thumb inner cub or, dense hold thug cold impel eight, sand lift a pulley furry earring rate comb fort.

Know, thumb height ease hull tan addle love lid aught her.

Summed haze, shed bay thinner riven ear all add-ins omen shoes soul overlay, heave hell deep lean luff wither. Him maid uppers mined two winner art. "Shoe wood endeavor mar a ewe" laughter smother "Shield aside tomb mar ear itch prints, inure knot won".

Bottle a din plea dead wither smother, four hurt ago tooth has salt on, in task foray sperm mission. "Yew conifer hymn orgy who ills a some age" his head. Win this hole tans haws omen edge who wills, he size let up-end hymn armored "A knee parson, hay belt toupee sat chore hand summer mount, mast biddy serving off thaw prints asses sand".

Buddies skimming add visor, thug rant fizzy ear, big game dispel eased, furry plant tomb harrier tour sewn sun. "Whim assed settle add in sum think differ cult who'd who, whiff Easter showers is swarthy off thaw prints ass". This salt on pandered ferret diamond thence head toothy womb man "Yew mast hell yours honey as tough etch for tea goal dimple eights, hover flawing width pressures tones, in curried bye for tea surf ants".

Win all add in whist hold, heat tucker slam panned drubbed, hand-out champed thaw genius head "Eye ham though gee knee off thaw lampoon yore mime aster. Water yew ash four?". Stray to weigh, all add in whizzer hounded bye joss a link surf ants, itch wither play tough pressures tones. All add in smother tuck thumb toothy pall lace, end win this salt on sore thumb, hew ass last forwards. "Lay tall no, the tall add in well lends fourth beak hauled prints all add in, ant tomb arrow hill marrow made otter, though prints ass. Lit oil ridge oyster marrow, infer river endeavor".

Minnie yappy ear slater, all add in anther prints ass swirl leaving a pill yin as some chewers pall lace. Furry weigh-in off are oaf flan, dinner ridden plays, though whack head was hard herd teller thaw fair ear itch prints, sand thaw tough all add in. "Hit mast bee hall lad in" heath ought "High mast goat hoof is it thumb, manse steel thaw lampoon thin isle beer itchy swell".

Wendy, all add in addle heft honor runt. Thaw whack head was hard as skies dims elf a sip pour pedal her, wither bask it offal amps. Hew win toothy kit shin, worthy made whisk leaning. Though was hard win tour, wither lamprey tending two off for newel amps far rolled. Wealthy made hid dent undies tanned hype rashers dull amp wore, sand gay vet toothy was hard.

Stray to whey, thaw was hard drubbed though lampoon ouch humped thaw gene Ian's head "Eye ham though gene knee off thaw lampoon your mime aster. Water yew ash four?" Twitch ear applied, "Train sport thaw pall lace, anther prints ass, two off our awful hand". Inner flashed whist ton.

Thin axed hay, though salt on whist hold hissed aught her add is up eared. Thaw skimming add visor, thug rant fizzy ears head "All add in a strict chew, end hymn mast bees heave ear lip pun ashed". Inner age, this salt under creed, the till add inch hood dye under neck stay.

Thought ounce peephole herd thin nuisance head "Know" big horse sea worse soap hop you'll are. This salt on pond heard forum home intended lass, teddy sided two shows sum myrrh say. "Ice wear isle finder" saddle add in "Handy fife ale, thin axe a cute mist traitor weigh". Soul a dunce hat doff, tool hook ferry's prince ass.

Buttered seamed thatch heed dizzy peered in tooth in hair. Hear hubbed is sand cinder spare. Buy axe hidden tear hubbed thaw wring. Inner flashy flight, though gene knee up eared, dandy held "Eye ham though gene knee off thaw wring, end your mime aster. Water yew ash four?".

Thud alight idyll a dunce head "Train support meat toothy prints ass" ant, inert rice, the wart hog heather hug gain. Winch shoe axe plane dub out thaw was hard, a lad anew a tad tubby dunce, hoe hip pastor's mall pack hat off poise on tour, untold hurt who slipper tint toothy was hearts trinkets upper.

"Wood shoe kerf awesome whine" shoes head toothy was hard, handy tuck thug lass ants wallowed a tall, end a mediate lid rapped head. Necks, tall add in burr stout offers side ink plays, sanders covered thaw lampoon ash elf. "You reel mast errors hear" hiss head "No takers await who ware wick aim fro" Mandy mediate lea, there hived dome.

Ever a buddy worst alighted. This old tanner range dig rate fees, tend thug runt fizzy ear when toughen wizen averse scene a gain, in thought hounds peephole ridge hoist inch eared, anthill thick hooch earn amour. In-sole add in, hand is prints ass, lift a pulley four reverend, wear every when tall add in tuck grate cared hook heap pestle ample hocked, inner cub herd, say flee a weigh.

Off hocks with outer tail … huff hay bull.

The scissor tail overpay in full lacks a dent, handle hot off pried. Hit tap end tour run fortune a tanner mill, whisk cold "Rain hard". Rein herd whiz off hocks, sandy haddock early tale, hub out wit she worse fairy feign. Heath ought a twist dumb hosted rack tough tail-ender four rest. Hew wood spindle hots off ours, jest brash ingot, anthill itch shown asp writer scold. Want error believe kneeing, why Lorraine hard crypt a round inner edge row, luck in forum heel, had red flax a dent append. Sud on leather wizard dragon filling honest ale, landau terror bull paint whore threw west hail.

Hymn mediate leer eel eyes, tatty head bean court inert rap. Hip olden heap hulled, an olive verse sadden though panes topped, untwist as may, rain hard sore wrist ale eyeing, annul is glow rein that rap. At worse sickle amity. "Define east end dumb host hatter active oxen thaw hurled, with outer tale" hymn owned "Aisle be camel a fin stalk, throw out olive deaf hocks as Cynthia would. Wattle ado?"

Thaw folks sleighed beckoned wandered watered who. Hick hood jests seethe wrest off thaw folks escrow wing, thumb in it there eel eyes hid luster spewed awful tale. "High note. Tales doughnut half two beat though backer tall. Icon where its tuft enemy at". Swede hid, handmaid us wait tooth thick leering, worthy haul lad third hail limb eating.

Is rain hard wen tick cross thick leer wringer rushed sigh lance felon aver rib buddy press ant. Hat hitter big hand tube bay herd. The none other than nun other, anthill livery folks whistle eyeing underground, inner stair wrecks.

Withers appear ear axe press shin, rain hard live teddies poor force high lance. Hear dressed these hem bowled folk says.

"A shoe or roller wear, hive bimbo lest wither fairies appear ear tale. At ale witch a very won add mire, sandwiches thus mar test tailor hound. Averse in sigh whistle lid elk hub, hive bin prowed two pullet or round hat though beck, button how that high miss ear for hay chain gent thesis sit. Eye dick wreath hat, tall focuses swill worth hurt ales Cynthia rats, worth herb you teak kin beef foolish own after thaw whirled. They surmise trick daughters".

Owe lather focuses luck to teach shudder, comb fused hand end out. Thin wants poke hop. "Olden numb in it. Witch who beck white sews appear ear, rough fewer rowan tailored knot bent horn oven at rap? Hide owned things hoe!".

Whinny reel iced hall laughter folks is sad note bin full dint hooch hop enough third hails, rain hard big game ash aimed, anchor hauled after though foreign doff thaw wooden did, four along, lung dime.

Anthem aural: Yukon full offer though peephole, olive thaw timer awl Arthur peephole, laugh other time, batch hook handful holler though peephole, olive there thyme.

This wine heard … over eat tail.

Wants thaw worse up rinse, hood aside daddy wood fined hymns hell fop rinse ass two head. His art worse setter pawn thud otter off though whimperer, sew witch host who've airy spatial presence, two winner art. Fir stir hose withers sent sews wheat, ate wood may queue for kettle yours arrow sand hills. Sick hand, wassail lid hulk ask it, tin witch's hat urn heighten gale, that's hang sews wheat, hit major art bill height.

Bat winch he soar though presence, though whimper oars totters tamp turf futon ridge hacked at thumb. "Eye dough won't hearse stew-pot flour, horrid hurt ill lid hull burred" this hell fish prints ass-head, withers cowl "Hype rough verge who'll sent ring kits". Though prints wood knot easel leg evince sew we win toothy hemp or oared rest ass up pissant ten tasked four ridge hob.

Thaw wimpy roars head "Icon own lay-off for youth edge hob asses wine heard, ant chew ill laugh toss leap withers wine." Soothe prints worse maid imp aerials wine heard, end wash own tooth his wine hurts oval, necks toothy picks ties, worry wood afters leap.

Well-off terrific stop pall though picks tie, this wine heard prints tarted may king hum eject hop, witch, wince pun, plaid thumb host love lea Walt says hump Olga's. Wealth, a prints ass won't head hit, tanned centre made defined outer mat chit wood caster bye. Winner made rat earned, shoe wish hocked. "This wine heard once twin tick hisses". Thaw prince ask who'd ample leave arrears. Wart touch eek! Wart hump hurt tenants! Bat thumb whore's sheath ought, thumb horse-shoe one tad hit. Sew fine alley, shag hay fin, end cave this wine heard thick hisses.

Neck stay, this wine heard maid up hot, twitch, a few he Ted's hum what her rennet, input churn hose tooth his team, yew woods niftier rumor a fall thumb eels, babbling hay wain thick hitch hands-off though pall ace, frame though wimpy roar's bank wet, toothy what arrays hoop off thick hitch un-made.

Hug hen, thistle lie prince a centre made two a squat pry sit wood cast. Thus thyme, shoe wish hocked two ear, a twist who hand read morgue hisses! Ferried his maid, sheath aught "Exit hair rubble think four upper incest ado, tuck hisses wine heard. Bat eye after avid, sew high mastic scepters dim hands".

Locking owe veer thick asshole parry pet, though impair oar sorrel hid hulk rowed, doubt cider ease picks ties, sinned one dourer watered worse solo bout. Hiss head "Water althea lay-dozen-weighting hop too? Won things once shod slipper croissant overlook." A verse soak wick laic wrapped a cross they hardened, whinny sorry sprints ass, anther pigment aching third when teeth amber race, ill host distemper end, wit allowed jellies tarted twit thumb withers tick.

"Waters though wide ear rough hole thus?" hear whored "Yard ask race fool, bother view. Gore weigh, yore ban ashed outer them pyre. Leaf know end done treat urn". Sew thistle eye prints assent this wine heard print, swirl act touts hide thick asshole waltz. "No otters two back hum mummy" whaled this hilly prints ass. "Off phone alley eyed suggest toothy prints, wile ahead itch ants."

Bat though prints wore snot hump rest. "Use hillock hurl" hair applied, bit early "Eye worse thought prints. Ewer rasp oiled lit hub rat. Hints Ted off up reach hating thug if tough arose, sandy knight inn gay, lieu won teddy's ill lit hop, panda use lisp hot. Hitch a roan due wing. Yam age herb-bed. Sawyer mast line knit", hand toffee road, of trees sewn can treat, hoof fine done otherwise sand scents sable parson two head.

Anthers hilly prints ass? Shoe whistle lefty loan, withered hop, harp hot, ingest whore mummeries fork hump a knee.

Thug lead dock cling … half airy dale.

Thaw ants swizzle ladle moth third dock. Shed sick sex sinner n'est pas stir read bedazzle overlay ass shook hood dope fur. Hit satin this hide oval idyll aisle and, dinners occluded corny rough if army hard. Shoes hat, hay off toured hay, pay chantilly weight infer thumb twat show pun. Fiver thumb wears maul land whitened numb bare sex wars larch errand abyss kit collar. Thumb other duct holders elf, knot two worrisome excel bead if her aunt, no wand egg hen.

Want hay, share deck rack, thin in other end on other. Hatch hick up eared, end won attar thyme, fife yell ouch hicks web horn. Thatch hicks snug hold on dearth thumb other swing, swarm hence a cure. "Want, tooth, reef, or fife" count head thumb other ducked whore's elf "wattle beekeeping numb bare sex" inches hatter's elfin toper fit a key pit worm.

Fair lass Sue, knit worst I'm fourth alas check tour rive. This yellow pinned, in doubt scram builder bay bitch hick. Batter check wizened as aims hero there cheques. The swan whisk hovered inner dulse soar tough luff, hand addle honks crony knack. Thus check worse knot knurliest eye near us deign teases broth horse in cyst hers, bat thumb moth hurl laughed immerse matches thaw restive arch hicks, sandal hooked aft rim, win olive thief army hard annum ills teas dumb.

"Ditch whoever seas hutch in hug liqueur reach her?" In knoll dense head turf rend. "Whale eye event, note aver" sure applied "Gore weigh, wean ever one terse he your hound de-rig gain". Pearl idyll crate sherry worse fairy a nappy, end a sided two runny whey.

Wand hearkens tore mean height, hick raptor weigh, why lever a buddy worse leaping. A weigh hurrah no verve feel dafter filled, dent hilly Wessex horse stud.

"Hide bet terraced fur rabbit" haze head, alter rims elfin fairy quack lea, ewers hassle leap. Tomb omens slay tarry whoa capped two filthy brethren annum elk humming outer van in whore mouse setter chores, fillet heath hand ruling a lover rim. Hit worse off ears wool found, bat tooth ill idyll dock clinks grater a leaf, alert hid worse slicker sedentary a weigh. Thud dock ling thawed "Eye hum sew waggly, evince hum fears toggle no teat meat, wood wrath a walker weigh".

Thin knee wad older whey, tool hook fearsome plays two collie zone. Knot furry whale lift annulled laid yonder check-ins sewer fairy hasp eatable. Sofa rash aught wily lift their, bat has thud haze pasty big hand tomb hiss thaw wateriness to din, whinny wore slit hole. Swanned hay, a fee wend, wither way vandal idyll tier.

Off terry wily note test though whether whist earning coal, Denis tart head whose know hob lizard. Late a wrist hopped, in, sadden lay, hissed rain John King camphor hum up-end disk high. Pea ring a pinto thick loud see-saw off lockers wan, scow winger wafer though inter. Saddle he, thud dock cling watch ton tilth hay dizzy peered, hands head "A phone lay hike hood gore swell. Bat twat width hose grays foal crate shores won't wither rug lick reach alike eye ham".

Swan eat rotted, dunce tumbling hick rosters know, weed is covered as mall ache, sore hounded bite haul reads. Bat watered his appointment. Thaw otter head beak home mice. Axe apt, trite tenders enter, thaw worse hat eye nip hatch owe otter. Deal light heady rant who wet, hence whammy hound for rages. Sloe lea, thick hold may dim tyre den hid as covered, twist as may, hick hood ankle lime how tinder though reads. Thence low leather rig all ling dock cling whist tuck, so roundhead buy sullied dice.

Lack hollyhock hind far more camp assed. Heap hick top though dock link hand to come beck comb, input hymnal idyll boxer long cider thief higher, ingot hymn worm income fordable. Fourth a necks sever ill wicks, cease topped wither farm errand dispute a full hinge hen rustle laid he. Thawed a cling roost wrong end hands home, bat mist knot halving up wrapper roam, mass see axe planed tooth hem.

Thaw inter big game asp ring off lowers, cheer happy burred sun warmed hays. Third dock wassail only ferry sewn kine, din stray chin outer swings, fount tourism maze meant, heat hook coffin when tap threw thick louts. His whooped town, end gay vicarious "hunk" answer priced dims elf. At worse he sway off sane "could buy". Hiss whooped angle eye dead thin furbelow, whisp potted ship cuffs once, spewed awful answer e'en.

Hill handed ants poke tooth hem. "Aye no why man hug lid dock cling, buttered wood big gratify cuddle liver hound ear, end wick hood beef rends". This once haul aft, ant's head "Yearn hot hug lea, ewe rob you tough holes wan!" handy luck titties ruffle action.... handy wars!

Thin haughty dog-end is reflex shone … Off hay bell.

Hair-raisers tore ear bough turn knotty lit old hog. Thus toggle laughed who spindle otter vest haze, hitting outs hide though boot chores, had my ring whole off thistle ices off suck you lance take, mount hence suffer reel it handle icing saw sages, enter hose oft haste itch hops. Our raft to rower, reed reamed a bout tough fees tough an whore mouse eyes. Want hay toothy necks, tease upper tight chest crew anchor who.

Thin wand hay, win though boot chair whistle hooking and earth thick count her, thin knotted hog's patients wren how tall over sadden. Wither ashen disk cuff fillet hooker grey chump, strayed threw thud whore. Hiss Easter leggy mutt on, endow weighed own thorough deaf lead. Though puerile boot chore aged, inch hook ask lever, batik hood ink ketchup.

"Eye double heave, these mast bee their itch a stand must suck you lentil leggy mutt on a knoll they whirled", thin knotty dogwood jell, two when he won hear ramp assed. Ah sere a gnome withers ill got in canes, hick cross tub ridge, handle hook in town, tour some maze mint, write their pea wring a teamster eighteen tweeze size, worsen a third hog … ended adder boon, jesters began upper ties inners he's worse.

Hew wars as town dead. "Hide battery leave hymn a vet" heady sided "Off Tyrol, to boon sir batter then won!". Hand inert rice, seed dope end uppers chores, hands napped grid alley. It chewed on tough beans uprising bat … image in niece apprise, whinny sewn boned rapped stray tin toothy what her.

Toothy doxy norm misters may, its hank outers heighten off lash, endear relies dotted whizzer affliction altered thyme. Sloe lay, heat rotted dome two whisk hen eland dressed teddy said honor spores, sin pond heard "Pear wraps eye worse tug reedy. Ice shoe differ rum membered, won bonus allot bet earthen nun".

Anthem aural hiss: big rate fool fur watch ergot.

Thaw wool fan third honky … Off able.

Want hay, third honky wore cap pinned aside head, haemostat end two break fussed, big horsy fealty mite belittle beat Hungary, lay tour own. Haste tarted tomb hooch a round, fallow wing up are thick

hood sea, end wondering for their own father fro misuse you'll play, sis.

Fare lasso knee founders elf enough heeled, worthy crass wore slush end Jew see. Beef furlong, third honky worse beseech you winger weigh, with outer Karen though whirled. Heed hid ant rear lice, quite lick reaping all hung an thug wrasse, their whiz owe Wilfred dyed hand ruling. Third honky prick tubby sears, ferry erred though Wilf's pause. Thud honky's head tombs elf "That sew wool phew wood probe hub lick hill meander rag mere wait twist denizen iced inner, bat own leaf eyelet hymn".

Win though Wilf's hounded vernier, third on kick white quite lease head "Eye wooden trite, off eye wore shoe". Wealthy Wilf setback inner maze meant. "Third honky shooed ant bee on-off raid" heath ought. Third honky axe planed.

"Ice tap ton earth horn" hiss head "Enough ewe wheat meat twills tick inure throw tube assure". Third honky when tone. "A fuel hike, isle left hop miff hoot, ant Yukon axed rack titter few one two. Thanet Kent heart chew".

Whale, thaw Wilf chest cud humble heave is hears. Ass third honky yelled a puss futon weighted pay chantilly, thaw Wilf adder though roll hook fourth earth hornbeak horse, heath ought, third honky whores bean stew pit. Button oath horn cutie sea.

Thin third honky salmon dap police inner gene, wither grate jelly gay vermin whore mask hick, witch maid though Wilf lie open tooth husk high. Doughnut elastic game, handle handed strayed inner thaw ambush. Asses hat their axe tract tenth horns, though Wilf mattered two whims elf "Knot hole lasses sore ass dimmers this seam" bat third honky jests mile datum, meant rotted a foam.

More roll: be where a fun axe pecked head fey verse.

Son know why tenth this event wharves …
Off-air wrist hoary.

Heiress Astoria bout all of league curlew worsen owners "no height". Nut big horseshoes relish aught, bat big whores hearse kin worse fairy-light. Annul hiker whack heads tape mutter, thick wean, hew whist hearken four bidding. Shell lift inner cars hole, wear thick wimp rack test twitch cur raft, big gauze, hints egret, shoe so wicker twitch.

Thick wean worse furry vein, end wizened fur in iced who hearse tapped otter, beg gorse no height wasp pick humming moor pewter fool, ever read hay. Sew ever rim awning, thick wean woods tanned lucky natters elf, inner luck ingle arson same "Mere ROM error, anther wallow west though fairies stuff asshole?" hand thumb error wood ripple eye, ever rim awning, wit know accept shin "Wallet shoe, mike wean, ewe Arthur fairy's tough thumb hole".

Bat wand hay, thick wean flue window at hairy ball raged, red faulty sea, one arm errors head, tour syrup rye sand his may "Wallet is on chew, mike wean, big horse chewed hays no heights berth daze sew shoes there must a tracked oven thick ink dome".

"Water lied who?" shoe ailed "High aft tubby thumb host boot a fool! Eye ham thick wean! Aye no! Oil ban assure in tooth hub lack for rest, far river endeavor, anther shield high". Thin thick weaned hooks no height often along jar knee, deepen tour darkens care he would, furrow hay. Shoal aft purse no height taller loan, width add hearken height upper roach in, hand wither grate storeroom jests tartan, inch he writ earned toothy pal hiss.

Purrs no height whisk haired, end big hand took awry. Shoes hob dance hob, don't ill shook hoods hob numb whore. "Owe" shoe whaled "Eye mauler lone end off whore wrist, Ivanhoe otter toad rink, hand naïf hood tweet. Aye Welsh hurl it high". Hits tardy terrain, at shilling winch hooked hub ranches, sands no height meadows elf's mauler shake hood, tooter right hook heap worm.

Shoe wore cap, ended worse thumb awning. Shoe worse scold, inch he wore sun grey. A lover sodden, sheep pecked top this hound off lit all feat. Pea ring threw thud hence sander grow, third alighted ice potted align off peep halter rot ingle long.

The worth this event wharves, sue wear under wait tooth thumb minds, worthies pent third hay mine hinge who wills. Ass thumb arched, wither shuffle sump hicks, this hang "Eye you, I owe, wits after war quick hoe", halt tug heathers them arched.

Wince no heights lip tout off tub ushers sadden lay, this event wharves squiggly dizzy peered in toothy yonder grow thin off right. This had curls hank toothy grown dent imp lord thumb "Police risk yummy, four-eyes shell parish, a few runny whey". Thin wan uttered I'm, this event wharves her rounded harm armor ring "Know wherries, mid-ear, welt ache airy view".

Thin the tolled hearth earn aims, switch wear "bash flap pig ramp peas knees asleep peed owe peahen dock". Thud wharf food hid mow stuff thought hawking whist hock, sin sewers hold dust handy whistle lead her. Docks head "Yew wood beaver recant tent withers, no heightened duke hence stair slung issue one two".

Welsh who whist deal light-headed wharf banned cud base sewn ice, inch he wars unit peas wither whirled. Hinders event wharves booty fool lid hulk hot age, shook hooked ink leaned, in, ash heat oiled, shoes hang towers elf "Wand aim eye prints walk home, dead undead damned, did hum.." end this event wharves swing tends milder teat shudder.

A freed hay, this hunch on, end thick hurl worse appear thin shed aver bin. Bat hole wars note Welbeck horse, backhand thaw pale ass, thick wean worse lucky natters elf inner luck ingle ass insane "Mere ROM error, anther wallow west though fairies stuff asshole?" In thumb errors head "Wallet is on chew, mike wean, big horse end off four rests, no heights ferric on tent, hence shoes tilth hum must a tracked oven thick ink dome".

Whale, thick wean whaled! "Shade hidden dyes. No heights tiller lie van dwell. Aisle laughter goat tour, tomb ache shower shed eyes". Sews shoddy skies terse elvers annulled womb an ant, aching wither hub ask it offer root, shoes hat orphanage hernia squiggly a chic hood. Off Tyrol hung jaw knee, thick wean rich stolid hill louse, swore shook hood ears no why two wars thin king gab outer prints, ashes hang towers elf "Want hay ma print swill comb". Thick wean tap ton thud whore, ant whence no height up-end hitch his whore annex hosted hold womb manse. No heights mild dough well commence head "Ewer whelk home grainy. Police scum mince traitor way, endeavored rink. You'll hook ferret hired".

Showers fairy kine, juicy. Wealthy whack head quince head "Think humidor tour, yaw ferric hind twin knolled grainy. Sway master award due. Plea stake the sap pullets wheat inch you see", thin sheep pastor rough root, witch shed poise hand hurl ear.

Sews no height hook hub heightened, big horse sit wasp poise hand, sheet humbled tooth hug round, inner comber. Thick wean winter wake hackle on tour sylph. "Wealth hats in endow vet haul. Know-all well no, the time though fairy stuff thumb hole". Bat winch sheer writ earned toothy pal ass, shed is covered the term error wish hatter, dinner Hun dread peace as since arrow hat watch heed hunt toes no height.

Beckon though four rest this event wharves sadder hive dome. Thick ride big horse hit seamed thatch he whist head, batch he wore sewn leers leap. Use sea, biff whore there hived, thug hood fore wrist ferries sad casters pillow verse no height, beak haws they'll loft hereto. This bells head "Shoe ill note dice, shoe alone less leap, on tiller ran sump rinse scum's took hisser". Of fairy lung thyme parsed. This event wharves sad luck Taft hearse no height. Shed bin laden herb heads, around did wet Jew ills end flour sever read hay, and this event wharves hang too rich knight. Thin, want hay, or ransom prints worse rye damp assed honor source. Hid dared teller fur boot a fool prints ass, hew worse sin on inch hunted slip. Hid bean tolled essay hung buoy, thought is testy knee whist whom harriers leaping prints ass, send cheek hood bee thaw won.

Hiss haw thick hot agent gut offer sore sin win tin thud whore. Win ease sore thick curl eyeing their, inner boot off older essence around head beef lowers, sick hood enter assist tit, tank hissed hair. Sadden laze no height wore cap, end owe pander ice. Shoe worse swell leg hen. Ever a buddy ridge hoist end maid up rose session tooth up pall lace furry whey, worm any ear sago, thick wean add groan olden dyed. Soar middle otter pump pence hairy monies no height whisk round ask wean, inch he, wither prints, rained form any ears. Hand big horseshoe us fair ridge any rust tour peephole, aver rib buddy whisk on tented, dinned olive topple lay-off a raft tour.

NURSE SORRY RYE MISS

Pasta meant source

Merry addle it all amiss
Fleas worse why toss know,
Endeavor, aware thought merry
When deal ham washer tug owe.
Wit fallow deer, two's cool, want hay,
Wish, whoa, sag, hence dare roulette
Maid ditch ill drain law, fan Plato,
Seal ambits cool.

Afar sites Tory

Ladle pall, if Lynn does
Atom hung these indoors,
Worming up riddle idyll tows,
Hoar madder Cayman cotter,
Ann weep Tillie doled ought tore,
Forcep oiling holler noise, nuke loathes.

Hung read hog

Oh well, madder hub art,
Show hen tether cub bared,
Tug adder purdah Gabon.
Bat twin shag at third echo bard wasp errand
Soothe upper dug hot nun.

Ladle tramp ate her

Lid oil bauble you, gamble owe a pure harness.
Ships endear mad art deco Cindy quorn.
Wear salad all buoy, outlook's aft Arthur's ship?
Asunder are haste tack fasters leap.

Block ship off turf Emily

Bar babble lacks ship, a view on a wall,
Yo, Surrey, yo, sort tree backs fool,
Wan fur dumb mast errand won four thud day
Mend 1 40 ladle buoy, Hugh leaves town, Elaine.

Haired abuttal host ship?

Lit elbow pea pa's luster ship,
Panders Santa, nowhere defined hum,
Leaf thumb owe loan, ninth ale comb ohm,
Wagon thaw tale spay hound dumb.

Oft' thaw all

Hamper to dump taciturn narwhal,
Hum petted empty, adder grate foal,
Annul decking sources, Ann oiled her kinks main,
Good hand pot tempt teeter, gather arcane.

Ladle Wally

Way wallowing quay, rants Troudeau tine,
Apes Tarzan dunce tears, sinners nigh to Goa
Nock a natty wonder succor rye nut though luck,
Harold, itch elder in, inner bad cess, paws stated lock.

At ale, bat note hail

Tree bland my strip land my
Sea high there, Ron, sea hide hair on,
The awl Arran aft two though firm ass, why
Fishy cat after tales wither curving nigh if,

Dud aver hue cease hatch earthing annual
I've ass tree bland demise?

Ticket hock take torque

Hick arid acre rid dock,
Thumb house rang optic lock,
Tickle oxter ruck wander mouthful town,
Nick hairy dick, horrid hock.

A wreck no foe beer

Ladle mass muff fits hat owner tough it,
Heater knock heard sound way,
A lank aim espied errands at town base cider,
Hand fry tinned mess more fit to weigh.

Loon or whore bit

Hated hit idyll, thick hat, underfed, ill,
Thick couch humped hover them, who won?
Though lit hauled ogle aft, who seize hatch fan
In thud ditch runny whey weather spun.

Burr duff hood fourth aught

Sin goes on gas expense, sup packet fuller high,
Foreign twin-tub lack bard spake Tina pay,
Wind harp I wore soap anther bards big hen tossing,
Worsen thought ordain tea ditch, two sit bee fourth aching.
Thick ink wizen thick cow ant ink cows, contain gout has mow nay,
Thick wean wizen though par law, heating bred a nanny,

Thumb aid wore sin thug hard on, an gain outer close,
Win all on game able hack burden packed toughen hose.

Haul up-end town

Check on chill, one tap though ill, tough edge up, halo, what, her?
Cheque felt town, in brow kiss crow, none chill comet humble hang aft her.
Abject cotton gnome dead rot has farce to see wore sable,
Hue winter paid, tum end as said, wee finicky rand brow in pay poor.

Up-end town wants moor

Other grant hole Jew cough Yorick, key head tenth house sand main,
Hymn arched thumb mapped tooth a tap other ill
Land hum marsh dumb townie gain,
Ant win the war hop, the war hop,
Ant win the ward own, the ward own,
Ant win the war own lay huff weigh hop
Though worn high the rap nerd own.

PO WET A CAMP ROSE
HAY HICK

None since big hat nuns hence

To wasp burr really ganders lie that hooves,
Did guy ring him Belinda weigh ball
Mum see worthy bar rig roves
Hand thumb murmur "wrath", shout "grape"!!

Be weird edge upper walk, mason,
That chores thought by tickle whores thick hatch,
Be weird edge hob job burden shandy
If roomiest band horse gnash.

Heat tuckers four pals hoard inn and,
Lung thyme theme Manx some phooey sots, arrested
Tea buy thaw tum dumb three,
Hence Tudor why length ought?

In dozen a fished aught his stewed,
Edge upper walk, wit ice of lame,
Game whiff all in threw thaw tall jay would
Dumb burr bulldoze set game.

Want to, went Owen, truant threw
Devour, pale, played, wants knickers knack,
Heal hefty Ted, on whither said, hie
Wend gall lump fin beck.

End as thus lane dodge upper walk?
Camp Tommy harms, maybe Amish buoy,
Over abject stay, cloak allay
Each hurdle dinners Joey.

To wasp burr really ganders lie that hooves,
Did guy ring him Belinda weigh ball
Mum see worthy bar rig roves
Hand thumb murmur "wrath", shout "grape"!!

Oh, Mark, I am row tit or ridge in alley

Thumb hoof ink vinegar rights.
Sand, halving grit, moo vis honor
Oil thigh pie at tea in witch,
Allure writ beck whore can sell offer lying.
Neural thigh tier swash outer whirred divot.

In tooth of alley …

"For width alight brag aid!"
Worse the rum and his maid?
Knot thaw these all jeers news hum win head blonde haired.

There's knot whom acre apply,
There snot tour ease on Wye,
There spot who dew in dye:
In tooth of alley of tether owed though sex sundered.
Can undo write-off thumb, canon tool heft tough thumb
Can on infer runt huff thumb, valid tenth hundred.

Thud home …

Insane ado dud cue black can
Estate leap leisure dumb duck Cree,
Wee Ralph, this acrid Revere anther
Hook have earns mesh your list demand
Hound tours unless see-sawed
Why's Fife my all suffer tile crowned
Wet waltz sent ours work hurdle drowned.

Foal an eyed holes …

"Mine aim as hussy Mandy ass, skiing off kinks:
Lucan may walks she might yonder spare!"
Gnaw thing bus side rim main.
Surround third deck cave
Thought callous all rick, band lesson berth
Alone handle evils hands to wretch furry weigh.

You ass deckle array shone oven dip end dance

Wine intercourse have yeoman off airs
Sit bay combs NASA, sorry,
Forewarn peep halter tease solve deep
All lit tickle ban, switch half
Cow-neck totem wizen udder,
Into issue mammon zippers, off dearth, disappear eight
Handy quell, stay shunt twitch
Zealous oven ate your hand,
Oven a chewers goad ten tight tolled
Emma descenders peck Todd-AO,
Pinny on serf monk, kinder a choir satay.
Shed éclair, deck cozy switch, impale damn tooth is apparition.
Wee holed east Ruth's, Toby sylph avid dent.
A tall manner Korea, Teddy quail, tatty ore
End owed, bide air crater, wits hurt
Tenor nail Ian hobble writes,
Atom on geyser lie, flipper tee
Hand thaw puss shoot owe a penis.
Gad Bill lissome Erica!

In a merry cannon thumb

Jose, canny whose sea, buy thud owns earl alight
What's up rowed lee wee ailed hat thought while light's lest glee mean?
Ooze Brad's tripe's ember rites tars, threw though pair alas fie tore …
… their rump arts wee washed, worse owe gallant least reaming?
In their rackets rag layer, though bum spur sting an ear
Cave up roof threw thin height the turf lag worse tilth air.
Jose, dough's thoughts tar span gold Ben Hur yacht way
For they'll hand off thaw Freon Theo muff though bar rave?

WELSH ACHES PEER
FOUR BIG INNERS

Solli/silly olly/soul all ... owed ham! Soliloquy

Tube beer knot tube bee, thaw test thick quiz tune.
Weather tease noble herring dumb mined, toss off
Her thistle ink sand arose avowed rages fort shun,
Whore toot ache corms again stays heaved rubble sand,
Buy up owe sing, and thumb.

Moor omelet

A lass per yore reckon new whim a ratio
Of fallow oven fan a chest, off mistakes silent fun see.
Heath burn meanness baccy, thou Sondheim's.
End know-how a burden, mime Madge nation at his!
May gore jar ice as a tit. He rung doe, slips debt hive keys, tie noon otter waft.
Weir bay urge hype snow? Ewer gambles? Yew worse honks?
Ewe wore fallacious Hoffmeyer ream meant, thought wear one toes hat thought able inner rower? Knot winnow, tomb muckier rowan, green ink, white chop for Len?
Nougat chew two maladies, chum bare on tailor, letter pain tan hinge tick Tooth's fever Seamus took ham; may curl effort hat.

Julie ... Ho! Seize her

Terry sat tied, India fearsome hen,
Wished ache on hat though flowed,
Leeds unto four tuna meted, hold dove hi'ya Jeff dull eye
Fuss bow-end inch yellow sand enemy series.
Answer chaff hull seer winnow waffle oat.
End whim mistake thick arrant wine hots surfs, sorrel ooze serve ensures.

Payer tension, Yule hot

France, romance, can't drayman land mere rears
Psych home two berries ease horn, otter prey some.
Though weevil data mend who lifts aft tore thumb,
Thug hood a soft hen turd whither boons
Owlet hit peewit seesaw. Then "Oh, Bill, brute".
As Seth tolled, uses ore, whiz home base, yes.

A fit worse sew, wit woes agree fuss fall
Tend grieves lee, a this ease errands soared hit.
Heron dour leaf huff brew to Sandy wrist,
Forbear root asses anon or rabble manse whore
The yawl, a lawn arable mink, oh my,
Toss pecans, seize horse few neural.

Hat Asian core

Wands, moron, tithe abridged e'er France, wants mower,
Claws though wallop withering lashed head,
Din piece terse, nodding sober comb sea manners,
Modus steal Nissan, hum miller tea,
Bedouin tea, plaster wore below sinner airs,
Denim, mate teddy, yak shorn off to tie go,
Stephan dozen, use salmon hop.
Dabble, lad.
Desk guy's furniture withered fever dredge.

Thus cot itch pulley

Myth ought a herd of ice, cries "leap, gnome whore",
Muck bath dose myrrh doors leap … thin ascends leaps.
Leap thought nit soap door have holds leave ark earth
Addeth hove itch diesel I've sorrel hay burr Sabbath

Barm a fort mines, grate neigh chewer sick concourse
Chuff nourish Huron lives off east

Hobble Bow Bell, Toy land rabble

Furs to itch:	Winch all wheat tree meter gay
	Ninth-hand hurl heightening whore an rein?
Sick hand which:	Windy hurl lay burr leased dun.
	Windy bet all's last end one.
Thorough twitch:	The twill beer thus sat toughs Hun..
Furs to itch:	Wear double lace?
Sick hand which:	A pun day he the …
Thorough twitch:	… their tomb eat wit Mick Beth
Furs to itch:	A calm, grim hole keen!
Sick hand which:	Paddy Coles.
Thorough twitch:	A nun!
Haul:	Fairy's foe land fowler's fare.
	Have her threw though fag-end fill the hair.

Amid Sam Morse fan to see

An oar Banquo rondo while time billows,
War hock slip sandy gnawed ink vile it crows
Sick white hover canoe, peed witless, shoes would buy in
Worse wheat mass crow says, sand wit heckle in Tyne,
Theirs leaps, tighten your summit tie, moved earn height,
Lolled end ease floors wood hand, says Sandy
Lighten dare dozen ache, trouser animal desk in,
Widow Haydn after rapper ferrying.

Store minute hiccough

Arrivals nowhere undead. This erector
Sassy four tolled shoe, earholes parrots
Under milled head, unto where, endeth in errand
Lick thaw bays loose firebrick, off these fish on,
Thick loud cop tours, thug urges pal asses
This hall lumped hemp holes, thick rate glow beats elf,
Yale, wet chitin hair itch elder solve,
Handle Ike though since abstains shall pay gent Fay did,
Leaf knotty wrack be high end.
Worse hutch tougher stream sour maiden,
Indoor ladle ivy surrounded widows leap.

FEY MUSS PEACHES

Rim member check kin a day …

Handsome eye fallow a merry cans:
Hassock knot watch chew work entry canned hoofer ewe,
Husk witch shoe canned who furry yak entry.
May follow city sins off though whirl
Desk gnaw twat a merry quelled hoofer U-boat
Twat hug heather, wick undo fourth off read dumb Oman.

Thug get us burger dress, Hay blink on.

Force core rinse heaven yours a gore feathers bar ought fourth Hun thus cone tenant an hue nay shun, can sieve din lee Bertie undead a gated tooth thee pro possession the tall manner Cree hate Teddy quail. Know wearing aged inner grates evil wore, Tess sting weather thought nay shun nor rennin hay shun sew cone sieved hand sew dead a Kate head cans hole long-hand ewer. Worm Etna grate Bottulph heeled oaf thought wore. Weave comet who'd head a cater poor shun oft hat fielders affine all wresting plaice forth hose Hugh hear give though lie vis thought thought nay shun mite Liv.

Utters all tug heather phut ting ant prop hearth hat wish hood due thus. Button alar juice hence, weak can knot dead Dick Kate, week an knot cons a crate, wick a knot hallo thus grind. Though bray vim hen, Liv van gained head whose trug ill deer of cons a crate edit Farah buff hour perp our two adder debt racked. Though hurled well idyll no tenor longer a member whoa tweeze hay ear, bat tit kin ever four get wot they'd hid ear. Utters four ass though Liv van graith hurt who bead head a Kate head hear tooth aeon finished walk witch the aye hoof ought ear hove this fairs owe no bully had vans.

Titters wrath are forest tube bee hear dead a Kate head tooth thug rate ask rum mane hing bee four ass—thought fro math ease a nor dad wit hake inn creased of ocean—tooth hat cores four witch thug heave thole assed fool masher roved avow shun—the twee hear hie leer a solve thought thee stead shell nut hove dyed inn vane, thought thus nay shun end erg hod shell haver gnu Bertha freed dumb, in thought Gavin meant off though peephole, bye though peephole, forth a peephole shell knot parish frame thaw worth.

Eye head did ream, Art tin lieu there keen

Eye yam map pit touch jaw win wit chew two deign watt twill goad own inn his story ass thug grate test demon stray shin Forfar reed dumb inn though whist hurry off fern hay shin.

Fife's core yours sinned hen hag Goa grate hum Eric can, in-house hymn ball lick shed owe whist tanned hood hay, sigh end thee Human sip pay shin Prow clam a shin. Thus mow men test agree Kay mass hug rate bee con lie tough hoe pet tomb ill Yens off nee grow sleigh vis sue wad beans hear din though flay miss off with ear-ring inn just ice. Sit Kay mass edge oh yes stay brick two wend they'll lawn go knight tough there capped ever tea.

Butt wan hand dread your slate hearth e'en knee grows tillers knot Freon. Nun dread yours slate hearth eel lie five thin knee grow west hills had leak rippled buy thumb Annie culls huffs hug rogation end though chins off disc rim a nation. Wan nun dread yours slate hearth e'en knee grow leaves Hun earl own lea eye land duff Poe Verity inn thumb hid stuff avast toe shin naff mat ear real prose parity. Wan Hun dread yours slate her, thin knee grow west hill anguish Chinon thick horn nurse off ham Eric can sews high yeti end fills hymns elf fan axe isle inner sewn lance. Hoe wee hove comb hereto date hood ram it eyes ash aim falcon dish on.

Inners hence wee hove comb tour nay shins cap hit till took ash itch heck. Wen though arc at heck 'tis offer rip hub lick rote thumb hag enough is sent whirred soft thick institution end thud deckle array shin off fin dip penned ants, the hay wears high nun up prow misery know two witch aver eye hum Eric can whist hoof all air.

Thin no 'twas up row miss the tall many Hess, Blake manners swell ass why tomb hen, wood big arrant teed thee Hun nail Ian Hubble rites off lie, flipper tea, end though purse sue tough a penis.

Sit a sob veers stud hay thought ham Erica hasty fault head don thus prow misery know tins afar ass hair city Zen sieve cholera cans earned. Inn stead off on a ring thus acre rid hobble leg gay shin, ham Erica hose govern thin knee grow peephole lab had chick, itch heck witch Chas comb hack mar kid "inns huff fish ant fans".

Bat we're off use tube a leave thought though ban cough just ices car wrapped. Weir off fuse tube a leave thought there oar inns efficient fans sin thug grate faults off hopper tune knit tea off thus neigh shin.

Sew weave comet hook ash thus chick—hatch heck though twill gyve huss a pond dumb end there itches off reed dome mend this heck hew ratty off just ice.

Weave all sew comb tooth hiss allow despot tour a mind ham Erica off though fear surge ant sea off enow. The suss know thyme twin gauge gin thee locks your eye off coo lin offer toot hake that rank will eye sinned rug off grudge you all lissome. No west though thyme tomb ache though prow misses oft hum mock curacy.

Know hiss though thyme tour eyes frame thud arc hand Esso late volley off Seeger rig hay shin toothy son loot pa though fray shell just ice. Know hiss though thyme tool eft turn hay shin frame thick wicks and suffer aye shell inn just ice two this sullied roc cuff broth there hood. Know hiss though thyme tomb ache just ice ear real lit tea feral love gads chill drain.

At wood beef fey till forth an hay shin two hover luck their gents sea off thumb hoe mint. The swell tour rings hummer off thin knee grows ledge it a mate disc on tent woolen knot parse sun till their risen envy go rating awe tum off reed hum end deck Wally tea.

Nigh on tins hicks teeth rhea hiss knot in hen nod, butter big inning. Tho' sew whooped hat thin knee groan kneed did tube low wafts team in twill know beak on ten twill hove air hood awe ache canning off thin hat shin rat earns tube is ness suss you shoe all.

Their wool bean either wrest naught rank Willie tea inner mare a car runt hill thin knee grow whiz grunted 'tis city Zen shipper heights. Thaw whorl wins off reeve holt twill can tin you tush ache though found hay shins offer neigh Chinon tilth hub right hay off just ice sum merges.

Bother hiss hum thin thought aim hosts hay tomb eye peephole whose tanned awn thew arm thrush old witch lids enter though pall lace off just ice. Inn though prose cess off gay nun ore rite full plaice whim most knot big hill tea off rung filled heeds. Letters knots eek toss hat is fie earth Hurst four fray dome bide rink kin frame thick upper bit turn ness sand hay tread. Whim mussed four river canned duck tours trug gallon though eye plain hoof dig knee tea end hiss supple lin. Whim mussed knot hall lower Cree ate hive prow test hood gin orate tint hoof his sick cull vial lance. Hug hain end hug hain whim mussed rice tooth thumb adjust tick hi Tess off meat tin fizzy cull fours wit sole fours.

Thumb halve all louse knew Millie tent sea witches sing Alf fed thin knee croak come you nit he mussed knot lid huss tour dissed rust off fall why it peephole, form any offer why it broth hers, says sever dents said buy there press ants ear toad hay, hove comet whore rear lies thought third dust any ass tide hop wee third Hess tinny. The hove cam tour real eyes thought there freed am mess sin axe trick cable eye bow end turf reed dome.

Weak can nut war clone. Ass wee work whim mast Mick though pull edge thought wish all all ways mar char head. Wick can knot earn beck. Their rare though sewer ass king thud a vote teas off sieve ill rites. "Wen well ewe bees hatters off hide?" Weaken ever bees hatters off hide ass slung ass thin knee grow whiz they've hick tome off thee Huns peak Hubble whore roars off pall lease brew tally tea.

Weaken ever bees hatters off hide ass slung ass orb buddies, savvy withy fat Teague oft ravel, can knot gay inn law gin inn thumb hotels off thee eye weigh end though owe tells off this hit tease. Weak can ever bees hatters off hide ass lung ass though knee grows bay sick mob hilly tease frame miss mauler get hoe two earl are jar won. Weak can ever bees hatters off hide ass lung ass arch hilled drain arse tripped off there's elf food end robed off third dig nutty buys sine stay tin "Four why 'tis own lea". Weak can knot bees hatters off hide ass lung ass sin knee grow win miss ass hippy can knot vow tend in knee grow win gnu Yorick bill heaves sea huss know thin four witch tough oat.

None hoe, wear knots hatters fie dinned wee well knot bees hatters fie done till just ice roles town lick what hers sand rite Chas ness lie come mite tease trim.

Eye ham knot ton mine full thoughts hum off ewe hove cam ear rout off grate riyals sand tree be Yule hay shins. Summer view hove comb for rash frame knar O.J.'ll sells. Summer view hove comb frame air rhea swear York west four fray dome lift chew bat toured buy this tore mess off purse hack you shin ends tag gored buy though hinds off paw lice brew tally tie. Ewe hove bin they've vet or runs off Cree hay tiffs offering. Can tin you two war rick withy fey thought Hun urn Ned's huff a ring hiss red dumped hove.

Gob hack two misses hippy, gob hack two wall lab ham awe, gob hack two sow with car owe liner, gob hack two jaw jeer, gob hack two Louie see Anna, gob hack two this slams sand get hoes offer gnaw thin sit haze, no wing thoughts hum how thus hit you way shin cannon well beach chain Jed. Lettuce knot wall low win thee volley off diss pear. Ice hate who ewe two dame eye fray hinds, sew weave in tho' whiff ace thud differ cult teas oft hood hay end tomb harrow, eyes till hovered ream. A 'tis sad reamed heap lea rue Ted inn thee hum Eric and ream.

Eye havered ream thought wand hay thus neigh shin wheel rice append love vowed that rue mean nun off fit screed: "Wee holed east Ruth's, Toby sylph avid dent. A tall manner Korea Teddy quell." Eye havered ream thought wand hay yawn though read ills off jaw jeer this Huns off for more sleigh vis sand this Huns off four more sleigh vow nurse swill bee hay ball toss hit town tug heather rat that hay ball off broth her hood.

Eye havered ream thought wand hay event thus Tate off misses hippy, estates well touring withy eat off hinge us Tess, well touring withy he tough fop Russian, well beat runs farmed inn tune owe hey Sis off reed hum end just ice.

Eye havered ream thought muff furl idyll chilled rain well wand hale haven nun hay shin worthy well knot badge Judd Jed buy thick collar rough there's kin butt buy thick con tent tough there car actor. Eye havered ream toad hay. Eye havered ream thought wand hay, Dow nun alley balm maw, withies fish us ray cysts, withies go vein or halving hiss slips stripping withy wards off inn tour position end knoll if hick hay shin; wand hay rite therein alley balm maul, idyll bill lack buoys sand bill lack gurls swill bee Abe Bill two joy inn ands whittle idyll Wyatt buoys sand Wyatt gurls ass hiss tours sand broth hers.

Eye havered ream toad hay. Eye havered ream thought wand hay aver reeve alleys shell bee axe halted, aver reel land mown tin shell beam aid loathe ruff plaices swill beam aid plane, end thick rook head plaices swill beam aids trait, tend thug lower eye off though lard shell beer rove eel dinned doll flash shell sea hit two gather.

Thus scissor rope. Thus cess though fey thought eye gob hack toothies oath wit. Withies fey though he well bee hay ball two hue how tough thumb mount hain oft a spare assed hone off hoop. Withies fey though he well bee hay ball toot runs farm though jungle ling disc chords off earn hay shin inn tour beaut awful sum funny off broth her rude.

Withies fey though he well bee hay ball two irk tug heather, two prey tug heather, toss trug gull tug heather, tug goat huge hail tug heather, toss tanned dap four fray dome tug heather, no wing thought twee well beef rhea wand hay.

The swill bee third hay wen gnaw will love gourds chilled rain well bee hay bell twos hing withy gnu me nun, "Mike can't rhea, toss off these wheat lend off lubber tea, off thee ice single. Hand worm eye feathers dyed, lend off though pill grooms pried, frame aver him mount inside, lit fray dome wring."

End duff ham Erica hiss tube bear grate nay shin thus mist beak home truce. Hole lit fray dumb bring frame though prod edge us sill taps off gnu hump sheer. Lit fray dumb bring frame thumb mite tea mount hains off gnu Yorick. Lit fray dumb bring frame though white tinning alley gunnies off pencil vein ear!

Lit fray dumb bring frame this know kept rookies off cull arid dough! Lit fray dumb bring frame thick her vicious lopes off cully faun year! Bat knot hone lea thought; lit fray dumb bring frame stow in mount tin off jaw jeer! Lit fray dumb bring frame luck out mount tin off tem ass sea!

Lit fray dumb bring frame a very ill land mow lull off misses hippy. Frame aver eye mount tins hide, lit fray dumb bring.

End whin thus sap pins, whin weal low fray domed touring, whin weal het tit touring frame aver reeve ill age end aver rhea ham lit, frame aver wrist hate tanned aver ryes hit tea, wee well bee Abe bull twos peed hop thought hay wain knoll love gourds chilled rain, bull lack main end why tomb hen, choose sand gent tiles, protest ants sand Kathy licks, swill bee Abe bull tow jawing ands ends hing inn though hordes off Theo willed knee grows poor cat you all, "Fray hat lost! Fray hat lost! Thin cod all my tea, wear fray hat lost!"

Though blowed, sweeten, tiers peach, Wins staunch arch hill

There rissole you shin: "Thought thus souse whelk hums though for may shin a fug hover mint rep resenting thee you knighted end flecks supple rissole verve thin neigh shin two prose acute thaw or witch her many two have hick Tory ask can clue shin."

Two farm men add Minnie stray shin off thus kale land camp laxities ass hear ear sunder taking a nits elf. Butt wear inn though prowl hymn an airy Fay's off wan off though grate test bottles sin his story. Wear inaction atom Minnie awe there pints—sin gnaw weigh end inn haul and—end wee after beep repaired din thumb edit Iranian. Thee hair bottle less cone tin you wing, end Minnie prep orations haft who beam aid ear rat tome.

Inn thus cry sassy thin Kay may beep hardened diff eyed who knotty dress though how's hat ten kneeling eth two'd hay, end eye hoe path hat ten eye off miff rends sand cowl leagues oar farmer cowl leagues whore rough acted buy though pole it tickle reek cans traction well may cowl all low winces four rainy lacquers hair Rimini wit witch chit hasp bean Esso Surrey two whacked.

Eyes hay two though how sassy Sid tomb any stairs sue huff joy end thus scuff a mint, tie hove gnaw thin two afar butt blowed, toy ill, tiers sends wet. Weave beef whore wrasse a gnawed ill off thumb host grieve ask hind. Weave beef whore wrasse men him men him man thus off straw glen hands offering.

Ewe hassock, waters sour police see? Eyes hay yet test who age wore bile and see yawned hair. Wherewithal lore mite end wit hall those string thug hod hiss governess, sand tow wage wore rug hence tum manse trussed heron knee Nev arse her past tin thud arc canned lamb mint table cattle hog a few mink rhyme. Thought hiss sour police say.

Ewe hassock, waters sour hay? Mike cannon sere run wan whirred. Data's vector he. Vector he a tall coasts vector he inns pie tough fault errors—vector he, ho wave earl hung end whored their rode maybe, four with hout vector he their risen hoe serve eye vole.

Lit thought beer real eyes Sid. Knows her vie vole fourth he bright ash hemp ire, knows her vie vole four awl thought though bright ash hemp ire Hess two'd four, knows her vie vole four thee orgy, though him pulse off though wages, thought monk hind shell mauve four word two word hiss coal.

Eye tick cup might ask inn buy ants sea yawned dope. Eye fee ills shore thought tour cores swill knot bees huff aired two fey lamb hangmen. Eye fee lint height held hat thus junk chewer, rat thus thyme, took lame thee hay doff awl end two's hay "cam thin, lettuce guff whore word tug heather wither you knight heads train kith."

'This pan ash harm madder', Hell is hobbit though fur wrist, toothy ingle ash harm me, 1588

Mile having peephole, weave bin purse waded buys home, thought arc hair full lovers safe tea, toot hake he'd Howe weak hum mitt tours elves two arm mid mull to chew wads, four fee ruffed wretch airy; butt eye ass your ewe, wide who knot diss ire tool eave two diss trussed may fate fell handle halving peephole.

Lot tire rants fee; rye hove vole weighs hoe bee hay I've dumb eyes elf thought, ton door gourd, eye hove plaice dumb itchy fists strung Kath end safe garden though low yell arts sand goo twill off mice objects. End their four eye yam cum hum manse chew wet thus thyme, knot ass form eye wreck rhea shin horse port, butt bee hing rice solved, din thumb hid stand eat off though bottle, tool I've whored eye hum angst chew wall; tool aid own, firm eye gourd, end four mike hing dumb, mend form eye peephole, may on her rand may blowed, event thud host.

Eye no why hove bat though buddy offer week hand fee bull womb an; bat eye hove though art offer kin gunned offer kin guff ingle hand two; wand thin cough howls corn thought par ma whores pain, gnaw runny prints off you rope, shoed hair twin vied though board hers off mayor elms: two witch, wrath her thin hinny diss owner shoed gar owe buy may, eye mice elf wilt hake cup harms; high mice elf Willoughby yore jenny rill, Judd Jan drew order off ever eye wan off fewer veer chews sin though filled.

Eye know-all ready, buy yore four word ness, thought chew hove diss served drew wards sand crow inns; sand weed who issue wear ewe, wan thaw horde offer prints, thus shell bead you'll leap aid ewe. Win thumb e'en mile hoot tenant jenny roll shell bean mist head, thin hum Nev veer prints comb handed amour know bull land whirr this object; knot Dow tin buyer row bead Dee ants tomb eye jenny roll, buy yore conk horde inn thick amp, penned buy yore velour inn though feel lid, wish hall shore Tillie hover fey mouse Victor he owe veer thee enemas off may gourd, off mike hing dumb, manned off may peephole.

Abed occasions peach, Head word VIII

Hat lawn glass tie hum Mabel two's hay off hue wards off may yawn. Eye haven ever one Ted two with old Denny think, button till know wit hiss knot bean cans tit you shin alley pass Sibyl four may toss peak. If you ours sago eye diss charged mile lest Jew tea ass kin gunned damp poorer, rand no thought eye hove beans acceded buy may broth hair, thud uke off Yorick, muff forest whirr does mast beat hood a Clare mile legions two whim. Thus eyed who wit haul may art. Yew wall no there ease sons switch hove imp hell lid mate tour announce thee thrown. Bat eye won chew two wanders tanned thought tin may king gap mime hind eyed hid knot four get thick Hun tree yore thee hemp pyre, witch, ass prints off whales sandal ate lea ass keen, Guy hove fort went tiff hive yours stride two surf.

Bat chew mast bull heave mew hen knight hell yew thought eye hove hound hit hymn paws supple took Harry thaw have he bird den offer ass ponce ability yawned two diss charge may Jew tease ass hick hing ass eye wood witch two dew wit hout though whelp ends up port off thaw womb man isle hove. End eye won shoot who no thought thud asses shin eye hove maid hiss bean Mayan end minor loan. Thus whiz Seth hing eye head two Judd gent hire leaf form eyes elf. Theo there purse son mows sneer lea cans earned hiss stride dope two they'll lass two purse wade meat toot ache cad differ runt coarse. Eye huff maid thus, thumb hosts sere yes diss sissy yawn off mile hive, phone lea up pun this sing gull thaw wit off watt wooden they Enderby Bess tough four awl.

Thus diss seize shin hiss bean maid lest tiff hack cult tomb he buy thus ewer knoll edge thought may broth hair, withies lung tray nun inn thee pub lick off airs off thus can tree end withies fie ink Wally tease, swill bee hay bill toot hake may plaice fourth with with hout tint eruption nor in jury two they'll hive end prow grass off though hemp hire. Randy hiss wan mat chill less bless sing, hinge hoy dub eyes sew men knee off ewe, wand knot beast towed don mere rap pie hum wit hiss why finch ill drain.

Jew ring this soured haze eye hove bean come fort head buy harm Madge's tea mime other rand buy may far mall lea. Thumb mini-stairs off thick rowan, end inn part hick you leer, missed herb old win, though pry mini-stare, hove all whey's tree Ted may wit falcon Sid oration. Their hiss Nev veer bean hinny cans tit you shin knolled if for rents bit wean mean thumb, mend bit wean mean parlay mint. Bread inn thick cans tit you shin awl tread dish shin buy miff other, ice shoed Nev veer hovel loud Den knees hutch is you tour ice. A verse hints sigh wasp prints off whales, sand lay tare Ron wen eye hock you pied thee thrown, eye hove bean tree Ted withy grate test kine Dennis buy awl claw sis off though peephole wear river eye hovel lift tour jaw kneed threw out thee hemp hire. Four thought eye ham fairy grate fool. Eye know caw wit tall tug heather pub lick off airs sand isle aid own may bird den.

Hit maybe summit I'm beef four eye rat earn tomb eye neigh tiff lend, bat ice shell all ways fall low though four tunes off though brutish rays sand hemp ire wit proof found enter rest, tanned effete ten knee thyme inn though few chewer Ike can beef hound off sir vice two hiss Madge's tea inner pry vet stay shin, ice shell knot fey. Land know, weal hove in uke hing. Eye wee Shaman dew, hiss peep-hole, lap penis sand prose parity withal may art. Gourd bliss shoe wall! Gourds sieve thick hing!

Thumb man row duck train, James manner owe 1823

Fallow city Zen's off this hen ate tanned how sieve rep resent tat hives:

Men knee import tents objects whelk lame yore rat tension Jew ring though press ant cess shin, off witch ice shell end ever tug hive, a neigh duff yore dull liberation, sedge huss tidier inn thus commune nick hay shin. Eye yonder take thus Jew tea wit duff feed ants, frame they've assed text tent off though winter rests son witch eye hove toot tree tanned off there grate time port hence two waver he poor shin off four you neon.

Eye ain't tour a net wit seal frame math though row convict shin thought their Nev veer whiz up peer Rio diss hints these tab lush mint offer evolution wen, rug garden thick Hun dish shone off this he veil iced whirled end hits bear ring up honest their whiz grate earn a cess city ford dove ocean inn pub licks her vents two there aspect hive Jew teas, sore fur veer chew, pat riot his sum, mend you new won inner cans tit you whence. Hat thaw prop hose all off there rush in imp peer real go for mint, maid threw thumb mini-stair off thee hemp are roar aside hing hear, awful poor rand inns truck shins hove bean trounce mitt head toothy mini-stair off thee you knight Ted's Tate sat sent pities berg tour range buy ham Mick Hubble nag owe sea hay shin their aspect haver heights sand dint rests off that tune hay shines son thin hearth whist cost off thus contain hint.

Ass him ill are prow pose all hiss bean maid buy hiss imp aerial Madge's tea off grate Breton, witch-hazel Ike why's bean hacks heeded two. Though go ferment tough thee you knight Ted's Tate cess binned a sire us buy thus fray handle lea prose heeding off man a fest sting thug rate vale you witch the haven never table hay hat hatched too thaw fray ends sheep off thee hemp error rend there's hole licit you'd took cult have eight though Bess ton durst handing withies go varmint.

Inn thud desk cushions stew witch the sin tourist huss give in ryes sand inn their range mints buy witch thumb hate ermine eight Theo Cajun has-been Judd Judd prop purr four ass hurting, gas up rinse sable lin witch there heights send din tourists off thee you knight heads Tate sore inn vole fed thought theme Eric can can't in ants, buy though rhea hand in dip penned ant canned dish shin witch the you've ass sue mud end mane Tay nor rinse fourth knot tube beak Huns Sid herd diss objects four few chewer Colin eyes hay shin buy hen knee you rope he Ann paw worse.

Sit worse stay Ted hat thick hum meant cement off they'll lest cess shone thought hug grate heifer 'twas thin may king inn spay nun poor chew gull two imp roof thick hand dish shone off thee peephole off the scant trees, sand thought tit up eared tube beak hand duck Ted wit axe tray whore din airy mod oration.

Hit kneed scare silly beer a market thought their assault hiss beans hove fur varied if a rent frame watt whiz thin ant Tessa pate head. Off a vents sin thought quart her off thug lobe, wit witch wee hove sew match chin tour coarse send frame witch weed arrive whore horror gin, weave all whey's bin angst schuss sand inter rested speck taters.

Thus city Zen's off thee you knight heads Tate's cheer rush sent a mints thumb host far end dilly inn fey viewer off they'll lubber tea end a penis off there fell low Menin thoughts hide off thee heckle antic.

Inn though worse off thee you rope Ian pours sin mutters reel eight hing two thumbs elves weave Nev her take kin hen eye parrot, gnaw doss sit camp port wither pall icy sew two'd who. Hit ass sewn lea winner rites sore inn faded door seer you sleigh men assed thought weir assent tin juries arm ache prep orations four roared a fence.

Withy move mints sin thus hem is fear wear roughen assess city moor ram media Tillie cone neck Ted, end bike horses switch mast bee yob via stew wall lin light tend dinned imp part shall lob servers. Thee pall lit tickles his stem off thee all eyed paw worse hisses ass sent Shelley duff arrant tin thus wrasse pecked frame thought tough hum Erica.

Thus differ ants prose seeds frame thought twitch accessed sin there ass pecked tiff go varmints; sand two thud a fence off hour rowan, witch hiss bean itch heaved buy they'll ass off sew match blowed end reassure, rend match whored buy thaw is dumb off there mow stun light end city Zen's, sand Hun door witch wee avenge hoy dun axe sampled fuller city, the sole neigh shun hissed a voted.

Wee oh wit, their four, took hand dour rand two theme Mick able reel lay shins sex hissed tin bat wean thee you knight Ted's Tate sand though spores chewed deck Clare thought wish hood cons Sid a runny hat tempt ton there par two axe tend there's his stem twin knee potin off thus semis fear ass deign jar us tour peas sands hay if tea.

Withy axis sting colon ease sore dip penned ant seas off hinny you rope Ian pour weave knot tint or feared dinned shell knot tine or fear. Bat wit thug hover mints sue hove deckle aired there rind up penned hints sand mane Tay end hit, hand hose sinned up penned hints weave, fun grate cons Sid oration end unjust print supple, sack no ledged, weak hood knot few hinny in tarp hose suss shun four they porpoise off hop press shin thumb, more can't rolling inn hinny owe there man nor third Hess tinny, buy hinny you rope Ian pour inn hinny owe their lied then ass thumb any fuss station off fin nun friend lea diss position tow words thee you knight Ted's Tate's.

Sin though wore bit wean though sun Hugo varmints ends pain weed deck layered dour newt rally tea hat that thyme off there wreck cog knee shin, end two thus weave add heard, end shell can tin you too add hear, prow vie dead notch hinge shell owe cur witch, chin thaw judge meant off thick compete tent awe though writ teas off thus go varmint, shell may cake Harry's pond inch chain John though parrot off thee you knight Ted's Tate sinned is pence able tooth airs heck you ratty.

They'll ate eve vents sins pain end port you gull shoe thought you rope pissed till Hun settled. Off thus imp aught ant fecht nose straw winger prow if Ken bee add juiced thin thought thee a lied pours shoed hove thaw tit prop purr, owe nun knee prints supple sat his factory two thumbs elves, two hove enter posed buy fours sin thin turn hell cons earns off spay in.

Two watt axe tents hutch enter position maybe car reed, don this aim prints supple, less sack west shin nun; witch hall inn dope penned ant pours who's go varmints stiffer frame there sore runt arrested, Dee van thaws mow west rim mote, hand shoe whirly nun moor sew thin thee you knight Ted's Tate's.

Sour pall lacey inn rig guard two you rope, witch whiz had opted a tan nearly stay Jove though whore switch hove soul lung a jet hated thought quart her off thug lobe, Nev ear thole Hess rum manes this aim, witch hiss, knot two winter fear inn thee hint turn knell cons earns off hinny off hits spores; took cons Sid dare thug go varmint duff act toe ass they'll ledge utter mate go varmint four huss; took hull two've ate friend leer ill lay shins buyer Frank, fir manned man lea Polly sea, meat tongue inn all-in stances thee jest clay aims off a very pour, sub mitt into win juries frame nun.

Button rig hard two though scone tin ants sir comes stances ore Remy nun Tillie hand cons pick you us lead if a rent.

Titties imp possible thought thee a lied pours shoed axe tend there pall lit tickles his stem two hinny poor chin off eye there con tin ant with hout tinned danger ring Gower piece send a penis; snore kin hinny wan bee leave thought tours other run breath a run, naff eft who thumbs elves, wood add opt tit tough there Rowan nick cord. A teak Willie imp possible, their four, thought wish hood bee holed Satch enter position inn hinny forum within difference.

Off wheel hook two thick home par rat hove string thinned rhea sources off spay in end thus knew go varmints, sand third hiss tense frame itch chow there, writ mast bee yob vie yes thought sheik can averse hub Jew thumb. Mitty's till thought troop holly sea off thee you knight Ted's Tate stool heave though par tease two thumbs elves, sin thaw hoop thought owe there pours swill purse sue this aim coarse.

Wit chews tug hoe tooth ham moo win, Jay off Kay 1962

Wee meat hat tack haul edge know Ted four knoll edge, inner sit-in know Ted fur prow grass, inners Tate know Ted fur string thinned whist hand a kneed off fall though rhea, four whim eat inn on our rough chain gin chow lunge, inner dick aid off hoe penned fee rhea nun aid Jove bow thin know ledge gin dig no rinse. Thug rate error knoll edge ink creases, thug rate error rig no rants son folds.

Diss pied this try king feck thought mow stuff this high inn tossed us thought thaw hurled hiss Severn own narrow live vent wore king two'd hay, diss pied though fecht thought thus neigh shins sewn scion tough hick man paw hour wrist Hubble ling aver eye 12 yours sinner ate off graw with moor thin there rhea thymes thought offer pope you'll hay shin ass or holed a spite thought they've assed stretchers off thee Hun no win end thee Hun Ann's sword dinned thee Hun Finney sheds till fair routs trip power cull active comp ray hen shun.

Gnome an kin fool eye grass paw fair rand howe fussed weave comb, bat conned dense a few hill though 50,000 yours off manse rack horde did his story inert thymes pan off butter huffs cent your he. Stay Ted inn the stir miss, wean no ferrule idyll lab out though forest 40 yours, axe cep tat thee yawned off thumb mad van said mannered lure nod two youse this kins off fanny mills took hover thumb. Thin hob out 10 yours sago, wonder thus tanned hard, ma gnome urged frame husk hay vis toucan struck toe there kine save shelled her.

Own lea 5 yours sag Oman lour rand tour height tanned you sack art wit weals. Christie Annie tea big annul Hess thin to yours sago. Though preen tin game thus your, rand thin Les thin tomb man thus sago, Jew ring the sole 50-yours pan off you man his story, this team minge in prove hide Dan knew sores off pour. Knew ton axe plow rid thumb inning off gravy tea. Lest man they'll heck trickle heights sent hell luff owns sand error plains beak aim move ale hobble. Lonely lass tweak dud weed have elope any sill on ant hell love is yawn end new clear pour, rand know a fame Erica's knew spay scruffs accedes sinner each chin venous, wee wall hovel littoral ear wretched thus tars biff whore mead knight tune height.

Thus cess orb wrath Tay king pays, sands hutch up ace can knot tell pot Cree ate knew wills asset diss pale sold, knew wig no rants, knew probe lambs, nude deign jaws. Shirley Theo pinning vest has huffs pace prow miss sigh coast sand herd sheep, suss willies hire a ward.

Suet 'tis knots up-rising thoughts hum wood haver stey wear wear rill idyll hunger tour wrist, two hate. Bat thus hit tea off few stun, thus Tate off taxes, thus can tree off thee you knight Ted's Tate's wizen hot billed buy though sue way Ted dinned wrested dinned witched tool hook bee hind thumb. Thus can tree whisk honk herd buy though sum hoofed four whirred—ends hoe ills pace. Will yum broad forts, peaking inn 1630 off thee found ding off though plum mouth bake colon knees, head thought tall grate tend on a rubble lack shuns arak hump a kneed wit grate duff a cult teas, sand bow thumb mast bee enter prize dinned hover comb wee than Sarah Bill cur rage.

Off thus caps you'll less story off hour prow grass titch ass suss sin a thing, git hiss thought ma ninnies cue west four no ledge end prow grass, sussed at ermine dinned can knot bead debt heard.

Thee axe plow ray shun naff spays swill goer head, weather wedge joy nun a torn hot, end ditties wan off thug rated ventures off fall thyme, mend known hay shin witch axe pecked stew bee though lieder off owe their neigh shuns scan axe pecked twos Tay bee hind inn thus rays furs pace.

Though souk aim biff whore ass maids her ten thought thus canter re-rowed though forest weaves off thin does trial river lotion, though fore's weaves off mode urn nun vent shun, end though forest weave off new clear pour, rand thus gin oration dozen knot tint tend two found her inn though beck quash off thick humming gauge off spays.

Whim e'en tube beer par tough fit—whim e'en tool heed debt. Four thee ayes off thaw hurled knoll hook hinders pace, two thumb moo nun toothy plan it spay yawned, end wee hove how wed thought wish shell knots seat go fanned buyer has tile flay guff cone quest, bat buyer ban nor rough rhea dumb end-piece.

Weave how'd thought wish shell knots seas pace fooled wit whip hones off master truck shun, bat within strew mints off knoll edge end hand durst handing.

Yacht they've owes off thus neigh shun ken known lea beef all fooled duff wee inn thus neigh shun ore furs tend, their four, wee inn tend tube beef furze. Din shore tour lee door ship pins high ensign dinned huss tree, hour ropes four piece sands sack your a tea, hoer rob legations tours elves a swell ass oath hers, solar acquire rust tum ache thus if fort, two salve this miss Tories, two soul love thumb four thug hood off fall Menin tube back hum thaw hurls lea dings pace-fair ring neigh shun.

Wheeze ate sale lawn thus knew see big horse their as gnu knoll ledge two big gay Ned, dinned knew rite stew bee one, end thumb massed bee one endues duff whore though prow grass offal peephole. Force pace high ants, sly canoe clears high ants sand awl tick knoll edgy, hiss know con shunts off fits sewn.

Weather writ twill big home off horse four guid door rill deep ends son Menin done leaf thee you knight heads Tate sock you pies up possession off Priam an hence scan wee helped a side weather thus knew owe shin Welby ass he off piece sore an newt terry fie yin the hater off wore.

Eyed who knots hay thought twee shoed door well Goan pro tack Ted Doug hence thee host aisle miss shoes huffs pace hinny moor thin wig hoe one prow tick Ted Doug hence to thee huss tile youse offal and horse he, bat eyes whose hay thoughts pace ken bee axe plow red dinned mast herd with hout fee ding though fie hers off wore, with hout rip eating thumb mist hakes thought manners maid din axe tending hiss Ritter hound thus glow biff hours.

Their hiss nose try fin know purr edge you'd diss, snow gnash anal cone flicked enow tours paces yeti. Eats has hard sour host tile two ass haul. Lets cone quest diss serves though bass stove vole mink hind, dinned dates sop poor tune neat tea four piece fool coo hopper ration man e'en aver comb hug gain.

Bat wise hums hay thumb boon? White shoes thus cess hour go will? Land thumb hay will lass caw hike lime though why esteem mount hain? Wye 35 yours sag off lie thee hat land tick? White toss rye splay taxes?

White shoes tug hoe tooth thumb hoon? Witch whose tug hoe tooth hum hoon inn thus dick aid undo thee oath her thins, knot big whores there he say, bat big horse there horde, big whores thought go all Will surf two organ eyes sand mesh your though Bess tough four hen ear gee sands kills, bee course thought shall lunges swan thought wear will lung two whack zapped, wan wear run will lung two prose pone, end wan witch wee inn tend two in, end Theo theirs stew.

Wit hiss four the sir ease inns thought eye rug guard thud a session lost your two-shift tower ref arts sins pace fro' mallow two Eiger ass sum hung thumb host Tim port ant diss seize shuns thought twill beam maid Jew ring mine come bin say inn though off fuss off though prissy dent sea.

Inn they'll lost 24 ours wee huffs e'en fuss hilly tease snow bee ink rhea hated fourth he grate test tend must camp lax axe plow rate shun inn manse his story. Weave felled thug rounds shaken thee hare shot herd buy that hest ting offers hat turn sea won boo stir hock hat, men eat thymes ass poor fool ass thee at lass switch lunched jungle hen, jenny rating pour rack quiver lent who 10,000 aught home mow bills wither rack seller ate horse son though flower. Weave sin this height wear fife if wan rock kit tinge inns, itch wan is poor fool asshole late tinge inns off this hat earn comb hind, Welby class turd tug heather tomb hake thee add van Sid's hat turn miss isle, lass cymbal dinner knew bill ding two bee billed a tick ape can have feral last haul lasso 48 stories truck chewer, wrasse why does ass hit tub lock, canned ass slung ass tool Len thus off thus filled.

With inn this lost 19 man thus sat list 45 sat alight save sir culled thee hearth. Sum 40 off thumb worm aid inn thee you knight Ted's Tate's off hum Erica end though wore farm whores off fist tick hated dins applied farm whore knoll edge toothy peephole off the whirled thin though save these hove yet tune yon.

Thumb Arran nurse pace croft know wan at sway two venous hiss thumb host tin trick hate tints Truman tin thee is Tory off spays sigh hints. Thee hack you're assay off thought show 'tis camp hair rubble two fie ring hum miss aisle fro' Mick ape can have feral end draw pin git tin thus te deum bet wean thee for tea hard lions.

Trance hits hat alights sore hell pin hour sheep sat see toss tear ass say fork horse. Tear Ross hat alights huff ghee van a sun price seed dented worn hing save hurry canes sands terms, sand twilled who this aim four four rest fire send dice burgs.

Weave adder fey ill yours, bats hoe hove owe there, seven off thud dune hot add mitt thumb. Manned thumb hay bill Hess pub lick. Tubby shore, wear bee hind, dinned Welby bee hind fours hum thyme inn mend fly it. Bat weed who knot tint end two stab a hind, dinned inn thus dick aid, wish hall may cup end mover head. Thug wrath off hours high ant says sand dead you Kay shin Welby inn rich shed bine you knoll edge offer you know verse sand envy Ron mint, bine newt heck knee cuss offal earning end map ping end hob serve hay shun, bine newt hulls end camp you terse four inn dust ream head diss sin, thee ohm a swell ass this cool. Tick nickel lin state you shins, hutch ass rye swill rip thee whore vest off this skeins. End, fine alley, this pace suffered hits elf, wiles Tillie nits sin fantasy, hiss sole red dick rhea hated hug grate numb her often gnu camp any sand tense off thou sends off nudge hobs. Pace end rill ate Ted dinned ass trees air jenny rating nude ham manned sin in vestment tans killed purse sun Nell, end inn thus hit tea end thus Tate, end thus ridge yawn, welsh hair grate lean thus grow with.

Watt whiz wants though fur thus tout posed don thee holed front hear off though whist twill bee thee fur thus tout posed don thee gnu front ear roughs high hence sends pace. Who stun, new worse hit tea off who stun, withies man Ned's pace croft cent her, well beak home thee art tough ale urge sigh ant iffy canned engine ear-ring come you nit tie. Jew ring thin axed 5 yours thin gnash anal heron naughty cull ends pace sad Minnie stray shun axe pecks two dabble thin Humber off scion tests sand engine ears sin thus hairier, two wink crease sits hout leys force all arise sand axe pence suss two $60 mullion nigh your; two win vests hum $60 mullion imp lantern lab horror tree face hilly teas; sand two dear wrecked torque hone tract four gnus pace heifer toss hoe veer $1 bill yin frame thus enter inn this hit tea. Tube assure, roll thus coasts ass sole hag rate dill off Manny. Thus yours pace bud jet ass though rhea thyme swat tit worse singe an

Newry 1961, end hit toss grater thin thus pace bud jet off though preview us sate yours comb hind. Thought bud jet knows tans sat $5,400 mullion aye ear—ass tag her rings hum, thaws hum witless thin whip hay four Ziggy rates ends agars sever a years. Pace axe penned at chewer wall ryes hum moor, frame 40 sense par purr sin purr weak two moor thin 50 sense owe eek four a very min, woo min inch aisled din thee you knight Ted's Tate's, four weave give hen thus prow grim ma hi gnash ion nil pry ore writ tea—event though eye reel eyes thought thus suss sins hum mash your enact off fey thinned fission, four weed who knot know no watt Benny fits saw eight Tess.

Bat tough eye wear two's hay, miff hello city Zen's, thought wish halls sinned tooth hum hoon, 240,000 my ills sway frame thick hunt roll stay shin inn you stun, age eye ant rock hit moor thin 300 fee toll, they'll link eth off thus phut bawl feel lid, maid off gnu met all alleys, hum off witch hove knot yacht bean nun vent head, cape Hubble off Stan ding he tans tresses aver all thymes moor thin hove aver bin axe peer rhea hence Sid, fit head tug heather wither price his yawn bet hearth thin thee fie nest what check harrying awl thee hack whip meant kneaded four prop pull shin, guy dance, can't roll, commune occasions, feud ends serve I've all, owe nun nun tried miss shun, two Anne nun known sell lest tea all buddy, yawned thin rat earn knit say flea two hearth, three hen touring though hat moss fear rats peed sew foe veer 25,000 my less spare our, core sing eater bout huff thought tough thee hat moss fear rough this Hun—all mows toss haw Tess sit hiss hear two'd hay—yawned who wall thus, sand duet rite, tanned duet forest beef whore thus dick aid hiss ow't—thin whim most bee bowled.

Eye yam thee wan whist dew wing gall though ark, sew wedge host wan chew two's take cull forum in it. How waver, eye thin queer go wing to-do wit, tend eye the ink thought whim host peewit kneads two beep aid. Eye dawned thank way yacht tow haste hinny moan knee, bat eye thank way yacht to-do though jab. Banned the swill bead Hun inn thud heck aid off this sick sties. Hit maybe dun wiles hum a few wars till he rats cool lit thus cull edge end you knee verse city. Hit twill bead Hun dew ring that arms off off ice off sum off thee peephole whose hit hear run thus plait farm. Bat a twill bead Hun. End hit twill bead dun biff whore thee yawned off thus dick aid.

And eye yam dill light head thought thus shoe knee verse city a splaying up art tin Pooh tin hum an awn thumb Moonies spurt offer grate neigh shin nil off fort off thee you night Ted's Tate's off hum Erica.

Men eye ears sago thug rate brute ash axe plow rear Jaw urge Mall lorry, woo whiz two dye awn moaned have a rest, whiz as kid wide hid hew ant took lime met. Hiss head, "big horse cities their."

Wells, paces their, end weir go wing took lime met, tanned thumb moan end though plan nets ore their, rand thin gnu hoe puss four knoll edge end piece sore their. Rand, their four, ass wheeze sits ale whisk gourd's bliss sing gone thumb host as hard us sand Dane Jew wrasse sand gray test add vent sure run witch manners sever rum barked.

Hat is rails hollow cost me more real, Poop jaw win pall II

Though wards off thee hain shan't Sam, ryes frame moor arts: "Eye hove big homc lie cab row kin vassal. Fye ear thaw is pairing off men knee—tear roar run aver ease hide—ass this skim tug heather rag hence tummy, ass the plait toot ache mile high if. Bat eye trussed din ewe, owl horde: eyes hay, 'ewe army gourd.'"

Inn thus plaice off mummeries, thumb hind end art tends hole fill in axe trim kneed fours high lens. High lens sin witch tour a member.

Sigh lance sin witch toot rye tomb aches hums hence off thumb mummeries switch cam flow dun beck. Sigh lance big horse their Arno herds straw wing a naff two dip lore that terry billed rage Eddie off this shower.

May yawn purse owe nil mummeries a rough fall thought tap panned whin thin at seas sock you pied pole hand Jew ring thaw whore. Ire rum member may chew wish fray ends sand nay burrs, sum off who whim pear rushed, why loath hers her vie fed.

Eye havoc home two-eye add fish hum tope hay hum age toothy mullions off chew wish peephole whose, tripped off aver eye thin, gasp Hess shell lea off who manned dig nit tea, worm ordered din thee hollow cost. Moor thin naff ass cent jury hasp assed, bat though mummeries rim maim.

Hear ass sit house fits send men knee oath harp laces sin your rope, wear aver comb buy thee heck owe off thee hart-wren dung lamb mints off sew men eye. Man, woo men end chill drain, Kray hout two huss frame thud hep paths off thee aura thought thin new. Hawk cane whiff ail tweed there Kray? Know wan ken four get tore rig gnaw watt tap pinned. Know win candy men ash hits kale.

Wee wash tour rim amber. Bat wee wash tour ram amber foray porpoise, neigh Emily two hence your thought Nev are rag hen wall level prow vale, acid hid forth thumb mullions off inner sent Vic Tim's off gnat sea is hum.

Howe cud men hove Satch hut her can tempt foreman? Big horse head retched thee paw ain't off can tempt four gourd. Hone lea hag odd lass eyed he all a gee cooed plain end car riot thee axe term a nation offer hole peephole.

Theo nor give vent who thee 'joss gent tiles' buy this Tate off is ray hell hat eye add fish hum four halving act Ted harrow wick lea two's have shoes, hummed Hyams toothy paw ain't off give hing there rowan lie vis, ass are wreck cog nation thought knot eve an inn thud hark cussed our hiss savor eel height axe tin go wished. Thought hiss Wye though Sam's sand thee ant hire buy bill, tho' hell owe wear off thee hue man cap a city four reeve hill, all sew prick lames thought weevil well knot hove they'll assed whirred.

Owe tough thud dap thus off pane ends harrow, though bee leave hearse art cry sow: "Tight rust tin ewe, whole horde. Ice hay, yew worm eye gourd."

Choose hand Chris tea Huns sheer ran hymn mince parry two wall pat Rimini, flawing frame gourd's elf-ref elation. Hour alleges teat chins sand dour spire it chew all axe Pirie ants dim hand thought wee you've ark home me villa wit goad. Weir a member, Bat know wit hinny diss ire four van gents ore ass Ann inn scent if two hate red. Four huss, two rim amber wrist hoop ray four peas sand just ice, sand took hum mitt tours elves two there cores. Sewn lea awe hurled hat piece, wit just ice four awl, Kenny void rip heating thumb ass takes sand terry bilk rhymes off though passed.

Ass bush hop off roam end suck cess sore rough thee up paws sill pee tore, eye ash earth edge who wish peephole thought thick Kath owe lick char rich, mow tough hated buy thug hasp pull awe oaf true thinned laugh, fanned buy know Polly tickle cons Sid orations, hiss dip lease had end buy though hay tread, axe off purse sick you shin end ass plays off fan teas hemi 'tis him dye wreck Ted hug hence it though chews bike wrist shins sat tinny thyme mend inn hinny plaice.

Thee char itch ridge acts ray seism inn hinny forum mass Aden Nile off thee hymn age off thick rhea hater inn hair rent tin aver eye who man bean.

Inn thus plaice off sole hymn rum member ants, eye fur vent Tillie prey thought towers harrow fourth hatter edge add he witch thee edge who wish peepholes offered inn thee 20th scent jury wall lid two a knew rill hay shin sheep bat wink wrist shins singe whose.

Letters spilled anew few chewer inn witch their Welby gnome whore rant edge who wish fee lung am hung Chris tea hence sore auntie Chris tea hen fee lung am hung choose, bat wrath her thumb you chew wall rasp pecked rack choir doff though sue wad whore thaw wonk rhea ate her handle horde, dinned luck two Abe raw ham ass sour cam in farther inn fey eth.

Thaw hurled mass teed though worn in thought combs stew wuss frame they've hick tums off thee hollow caused, dinned frame that test Tim money off this halve hive hers. Hear ratty add fish hum thumb mammary live son, end burn sits elf on tour soles. Sit may cuss husk rye hout: "eye ear thaw hiss purring off men knee—tear roar run aver eyes hide—bat tight rust tin ewe, owl horde: ice hay, ewe army gourd."

Stan dope forum Eric cab eth chop men

Aim ear two knight big horse Menin whim men off thee you knight Ted's Tate's Millie Terry hove gay van there lie vis form miff red dumb. Eye yam knot eared an height big horse Share roll craw, Row sea owed on nail, Mar tins she inn, Jaw urge clue knee, Jay inn fonder roar Fill done a hew, sack rough iced there lie vis form he.

Off mime hem Harry surfs Mick or wreck Tillie, hit whiz knot move east tars awe mew sessions, bat thee you knight Ted's Tate's Millie tarry hoof aught ton this yours off he whoa gee ma, thatch angles off yet numb, end though bitches off nor Mandy. Two knight eyes hay wish hoods a port thee Press add dent tough thee you knight Ted's Tate's sand thee you ass Millie tarry ant healthy lubber alter he hogging, Burke inns talk were ring, hip heat eyed hide lubber hills tug home ache therm who vie send mew sick canned wines hum wear hells.

Oft a roll, laugh they'll lift tin ear rack, the wood dent bee all loud thee fried home muffs peach their bean giver near two'd hay. Eye Ron Nick Lee, the wood bee Pooh two'd eth that thee ands off Sad ham Huss Seine nor Owes Sam a bun Lad din.

Eye wont who no wow they've airy peephole whore rug ants wore big horse off thole lass offal hive, kin passable lea bee this aim peephole whore four rub bore shun? They ore this aim peephole whore fur ran a mall writes bat again nest their heights off thee Hun borne.

Thumb move hissed tars hay the won't tug hoe two eye rack end surface 'who men she'll diss' forth ear rack keys. Eyes sail het thumb higher wan weight hick kit tend Goa.

Know wan lie cuss though whore. Bat thaw Hun thin gay hay tomb whore hiss thee effect thought thus can't rhea hiss bean four Sid dint who whore—inn ascent peephole hovel host there lie vis—end their, bat forth thug race off gourd debt cooed hove bin numb eye broth hum eye huss binned door raven wars me yawns Hun.

Hun Diss ember 7, 1941, their rare know wreck hordes off move ease tars tray dung though blaze sing what hearse off purl arbor.

Runs apt ember 11, 2001, their rare know pick chewers off move ease tars tan dung gas 'you men shill lids' hug hence Sid thud dab Brie yawned foaling buddies ass ending frame though hurled raids hen tower. Their wear roan leap hole lease men end fie are men—nun door pay head sieve ill serve ants hug....

.... . owe, eye canned bee both erred wit ten hay mower off thus auntie haul lea would die a tribe!!!

... in off, fall red eye!!

Wrasse pond in tool hand my inns, Prints hissed high Anna, 1997

Laid ease sand gin tall men,

Aim host big yin buys hay yin howe worm lea eye will comb thus cone for ants son lend my inns can vein do buy thumb my ness sad visor rhea grew panned though lend my inns serve I've horse gnat war.

Kit hiss hoe well comb big horse thaw hurled dust tool idyll owe hair rough though haste off fly, flea Mendel and witch auntie-purse a knell hand my inns arc horse sing ham hung sum off thee pour wrist peephole own hearth.

And heed, dun till major knee two Wan goal law wear lea thus sheer—Ron witch eye ham go wing two's peak thus more nun—eye whiz lar jelly honey wear off fit two. Foray my inn ness ass tell thick ill lore. Lung gaff torque un-flecked hiss send dead, hits sin no sent Vic Tim's dye ore roar one did sing lea, ink can't tries off witch wee hurl idyll. There loan leaf ate hiss Nev air rip port head.

Though hurled, wee thoughts men knee awe there pray hock you patients, rum manes lard jelly Hun moo vid buy herd eth thrall loves sum thin lie Kate hand red peephole aver ream anthem—any off thumb wee men end chilled drain.

Though sewer knot kilt tout write—tanned the numb burr run other 1,200 arm on eth—so far terry bill hinge juries sander hand dick capped furl lie.

Fie worse sin hang owe la inn Jan new hurry wit their head craws—sick Hun tree wear their rare 15 mullion lend my inns sinner pop you'll hay shun, laid ease sand gent tall men, off 10 mullion—wit thud as ire oft rowing whirled debt tension two thus vie tall, bat tea there two lar jelly niggle acted tissue.

Sump peephole chews twin tarp writ may visa 'tis hay poll it tickle state meant. Bat hit wuss snot. High ham note tap holly tickle fig your. Ass eyes head debt though thyme, end eyed lick tour he iterate know, may enter rests sore human at Aryan. Thought ass Wye eye fault rowan tooth hiss hew man tread Judd he.

The suss Wye eye one Ted two pull aid own may par tin wore king toe words saw hurled why Yid barn Hun this whip hones. Jew ring maid hays sin hang go lore, eyes haw what fur stand though rhea ass picks off thus cur. Gin thee horse piddles offal you wander, thick cap pot hill, land who am bow, seen off bit her fie tongue knot lung gag hoe, I've is a Ted's hum off them mien Vic Tim's sue heads serve hived, ends haw there inn juries. Eye ham knot go wing two'd ascribe thumb, big horse sin may axe Perry ants sit earns tomb any peephole aweigh frame this objects. Off ice two's hay, thought whin Yule hook cat thumb angled buddies, hum off thumb chill drink aught buy thus my inns, ewe mar villa to there serve high vole.

Water soak rue well lab bout the sin juries, hiss thought the yore all mows tin very able less offered, worm head dick hill rhea sources arse cares. Eye hob served four mice elf sum off thee hobs tickles two imp roofing mad dick hulk air inn mows tough the sauce spittle's. Oft ten their hiss sick Ron hick short edge off mad diss sin, off pane kill hearse, seven off Anna's that hicks.

Surge inns cone stint lea yen gauged inn amp you Tate hing shat turd limns, Nev ear hove vole thee face hilly teas wee wood axe pecked two sea hear. Sew thee ewe man pane thought hast who be born hiss oft ten bee yawned dim Madge an inn. The sum merge antsy mad dick hulk air, mow rover, hiss sewn lea though furs tip beck tours aught off lie. Forth hose who's loving hiss they'll hand, lass off fin harm moral egg, hiss sin owe veer well Ming handy cap witch lusts furl lie if.

Eyesore though fie in wore cub bean dun buy there head craws sand a there rage antsy stew rip lace lust limns. Bat may king prose that ticks sissy cast lea ass willies sack hump lick hated busy ness. Four axe sample; lay hunch aisled well kneads ever old if a rent fit tins ass sit grew solder. Sump thymes, this ever writ tea off thin Jewry may kiss though fit tin off fin art official him imp paws sable. Their earn ever run naff free sources tour hip lace soul though limns thought hurl lust. Ass there head craws hove axe pressed tit : 'teach Vic Tim whose surf hives, swill ink hurl lie fit thyme axe pence's furs urge jury yawned prose that ticks scare tow tilling bat wean 2,000 dinned 3,000.'Thought 'tis Ann nine toll a rabble lode four awe hand dick apt purse sin inner pour can't tree. Thought hiss hum thin twitch though whirled shoe dirge ant hilly tern knits cons shan't.

Sin hang owe law wan nun ever rhea 334 mambas off though pope you lay shin hiss inn amp you tea! Hang go la hiss thaw hi assed trait off amp you teas sin thaw hurled. Howe Cancun trees switch man you fact chewer rand trayed din the sway ponce queer there conch hence wits hutch who manned ever station?

May there'd mane axe Perry ants whist whose he watt hiss bean dunce, lowly end Perry loss lea, tug het this my ness outer thee hearth. Inn thick wheat hoe wand who am boar reed gin eyes pent hum awning withers maul teem frame hay lout rust, twitch a straining hang owe lance two wear con though purvey sieve my inn feel lids hands hoop purr vie sing there war. Kiss peak off 'four teem' big horse mean off thumb hinds sad visor rig roup—poor, run thus sin stance, thee hay lout rust—two vole lint tear four thus has hard us wore car you sue alley four more mambas off four rowans her vices.

Eight hake the sop part tune nutty two pear mite rib Ute two though ark this mend who wan hour bee half—though payrolls the yin counter rare knot jest can find two my inns. Tomb embers off thumb my inns sad visor rig croup teem ink ham bode ear, Chris Howes and Houn Horth, work hid knapped buy thick Emir rue jaw your rag hoe wand their fey tease Hun sir ten. Wick cannon lea prey four there say fret earn.

Match ingénue witty hiss Conan tomb aching sum off this my inns. Men neared as signed toot rap Ann nun wear rhea deem-minor. Whin never Satch hat Ricky my inns sup ear, thud deem-minor whelk all inn wan off this hoop perve icing teem, hew ill thinned hake cover.

Thought a swat kips there lie vis perp pet shoe alley yacht wrasse. Kit mite Bill Hess has hard diss, sigh rough lack Ted, dafter mauve is sit two wan go laugh sum off that heck nickels kills sue Sid din may king my inns sad bean up plied tub bat hum eth hods off rim hoof fin thumb. Men nay off this my inns ore relate Tivoli cheep—the ache kin bee boat fur 5 up peace sorrel Hess. Tray sing thumb, luff tin thumb, end is posing off thumb, coasts farm whore—summit thymes sis match ass say Hun dread thymes mower.

Rang hoe la hiss fool love ref huge he's rat earning aft her all Hong wore. The hay prison ton other asp pecked off thus trad Judd he. There riff you gee terns two words some, off ten ignore rant off conned is shins inners sew mill hand. Hun nose off my inns, bat tome word bow end, digger ness took home pleat thee jar knee gits though bet her off hymn. Ore huff hinds my inns son watt whiz wants hustle and, end at hemps took leer thumb. Their worm any axe hemp pills off thought tin hang awe la. This my inns sin flicked mow stuff there cashew all tease son peephole hew wart rye hing tomb eat thee Ellie men terry kneads offal lie if. This trike thaw high, forth hug rand mow there, gather ring fie are would fork hooking—the ham bush thatch aisled sinned two cull act what her four thief homily.

Eye whiz imp pressed two seethe owe ark bee yin dun buy men hay off thaw hurled sage ants ease son 'my know air ness'. Off chilled ran kin beat aught hats cool, luff fad dolts kin bee hell pit tool earn watt to-do, wand watt knot to-do winner he gins thought tough bin my end, thin life scan bees say vid dinned in juries red used.

Their arse head tube beer hound 110 mullion my inns slur king sum wear inn though whirled—dinned owe veer wrath herd off thumb mar two beef hound in-off free car! Hang hole ha hiss probe ably moor revel lea my end thin hinny wear hells, big horse though wore when ton four Satch ill lung thyme, mend hit tin faded sew match off thick Hun tree. Sew thought can tree ass go wing two bee inn fest head wit my inns, sand wells huffer men knee moor Vic Tim's. Sand thus springs meat who wan off thumb mane can clue shins eye retched aft her thus sex Perry ants.

Eve in naff thaw hurled diss hided tomb arrow tube Anthea's whip puns, thus terry bill leg ass sea off my inns sole red deign thee hearth wood can tin you two play hug thee pour neigh shuns off thug lobe. 'Though weevil thought mend who'll loves softer thumb. End sew wit seams stew myth air wrests ass hurt in knob legation up on there wrest tough fuss. Wan off may hob Jack tiffs sin viz a tin hang hole ha waste who four word thick cores off though, slake their head craws, try van inn thin aim off who man nutty two sack cure ran in turn gnash shun Alban awn this whip puns. Sins thin, wear clad two sea, sum reel prow grass hiss bean maid.

Their roars hinds offer chain Jove art—hat lease tins hum parrots off thaw hurled. Four thought wheeze shoed beak awe schuss lea grate fool. Huff fin hinter gnash shun Alban nun my inns kin bees sick cured debt mince, loo king Farah head, thought thaw hurled maybe ass saver plaice four thus jenny ray shuns ground chilled run.

Bat four thus jenny ray shun inn match off thud dove eloping whirled, their Welby know rill leaf, know rill lack session. That whole oft eths sand inn Jerry's coursed buy my inns sole red dither, whelk hunt tin you. Thus stray sing end live ting guff my inns, ass eyes haw win hang hole ha hiss sad diss parrot lease low busy ness. Sew win may mined ass enter all quest shin rum manes. Shoed wean knot doom whore took wick in thud he minors' swear cut who whelp thee in Jew whirred beck two-some sore tough live, two fur there hour hone country boo shin two wade dinned devil lope mint?

Thick Hun tree sinner itched buy though whirr rocked Hun buy hits sow verse sees sage gent seas sand nun go varmint all organ eyes say shuns, sew auk two hell peephole lin off Rick awe wand haze yurt who wimp roof thick Wally tea off there life. Shat my inns costar cans tint shed owe owe verse sew match off thus whirr. Crease settle mint offer a few gee suss maid moor has hard us. Gude lawn diss putt tout off bow ends. Wreak cover riff rum wore hissed allayed. Hayed war curse thumbs elves harp hut tat rusk.

Eye wood lick two sea moor dun four though sill loving inn thus 'snowmen's lawned' witch lice bat wean there Hongs off yes turd hay end thee your gent kneads off two'd hay. Eye thank wee oh wit. Eye hall sew thin kit wood bee off Benny foot who a Saul, ass swill ass two thumb. Thumb whore racks spud dish schuss lea weak kin hand thus play gone hearth cost buy they'll hand my inn, thumb whore head dilly kin wheeze het a bout thick Huns trucked toughed asks two witch sew money gyve there rand inn thick horse off human knit tea.

Awn thud eth off Prints hissed high Anna, Ill his hob eth II, 1997

Sins lost son dazed red fool noose wee hove scene, threw hout Brit Hun end or row wind thaw whirled, din owe fur well Ming axe press shun off sudden ness hat die Anna hissed eth.

Weave haul bent wry inner duff errant waist hook hope. Pities snot tease eat who axe pressers hence off laws, hence thee inn knish shell shack hiss oft tin suck seeded buy hum hicks stewer off father fee lungs : diss bee leaf, fink hum prey hence shun, angora—end cons urn four though sewer rum mane

Wee hove vole fill though seam motions inn the solace to feud hays. Sew watt eyes hay two ewe know, ass sure Quinn end ass sag random other, ice hay frame eye hart.

Fur, sty went two pate rib Ute two die Anna mice elf. Shoe wizen axe hep shin knoll land give Ted who man bean. Nun gude thymes sand bed, sheen ever last hark up asset heat who's mile end luff, gnaw two wins pyre wrath hers wither worm thinned kine Dennis.

Eyed mired dinned dross peck Ted whore—fur hair wren urge he yawned comb mitt mint two a there, Sandy's pay shall lea four herd avow shun tour too buoys.

Thus weak cat Bill moral, weave fall bent rye into whelp will yum end hairy cam toot harms withy deaf fist hating laws thought the yawned their wrest tough fuss sieves offered. Know wan noon nude die Anna well lover four get hair. Mullions off fathers soon ever matter, bat felled thin newer, well rum ember hair.

I've whore wan bill heave thought the rare less sins tube bead ran win frame thee axed roared in hairy yawned move inner he axe shunt who herd eth. Ice sheer run ewer deter my nation touch airy share mammary.

Thus sis soul sew inn up port you nutty form he, yawn bee half off muff homily, yawned a special leap rinse chore ills sand well yum end hairy, tooth hank call off ewe hoof brat flours, scent mess ages, hand pager aspects sins sew men knee waist who are rum ark Hubble purse on.

The sacks off kine din ness save bin awe Hugh Jess horse off hell panned come fort. Earth hots sore all sew wit die Anne's fame hilly end though fame hilly soft hose who'd eyed wither. Eye no thought the two hove drowns string eth frame watt hose sap pinned sense lost tweak hen, diss the sick two wheel there soar rowan thin two-faced huff few chewer with hout till huffed wan.

Eye hop thought tomb arrow weaken haul, wear river wear, joy nun axe press sing hour Graiae fat die Anne ass loose, sing ratty chewed four hair roll two shore till hive. Fit hiss itch hence two Shaw two thee hole whirled though Brit tush neigh shin you knighted dung reef fender aspect.

No bell pries peach, Moth hurt her ease awe, 1979

Ass weave gat herd deer tug heather tooth hank gourd forth a know bell piece pries eye thin kit twill bee boo tough hell thought weep ray thee prey a rough sent France hiss off ass sea see witch haul weighs her prizes Smee fairy match—whip ray thus prey her ever rid hay off tore wholly come you Neon, big horse cities fairy fit tin four reach wan off fuss, sand eye haul whey swan door thought 4-500 your sago was sent France hiss sofas sea see camp hosed thus prey hour thought the hid this aim duff faculties thought weave two'd hay, ass wick hump hose thus prey air thought phuts fairy nigh's leaf our rustle sew. Eye thin cuss hum off ewe wall red dye hove gat tit—sew wee well prey tug heather.

Lettuce than neck gourd four thee hopper chew nutty thought weal hove tug heather two'd hay, four thus guff tough piece thought rum hinds suss thought weave bin Cree hated tool hove thought piece, sand gee suss big game an tube ring thought gude noose two though pure.

Hebe he yin gourd big game an inn awl thin guess lie cuss axe sipped seen, end hip row claimed ferric leer lea thought tea hid cam tug heave thee gude noose.

The noose whiz piece towel love gude Will end thus suss hum thin thought weal wont—thee piece off hart—tanned gourd loft though whirled sew match thought Teague gay vis sun—nit whiz sag ghee van—nit Tess suss match ass a fit whose hay hit heart gourd tug hive, big horse seal luffed though whirled sew match thought Teague Avis Hun, end dig hay vim two verge inn merry, yawned watt dead shoe dew eth hymn?

Ass sue ness hick aim mint two hurl eye—fame media Tillie shoe when tin hay stew gyve thought gude knew, sand ass sheik aim inn tooth a how's suffer cuss sin, thee chilled—thee Hun borne chilled—thee chilled din thew whom off all Izzy bath, lipped witch hoy. Hew Oz though till idyll Hun borne chilled, wiz though forest mess singe your off piece.

Here wreck hogan iced though prints off piece, seer wreck hogan iced thought cries task home tube ring though gude noose four ewe wand mean. Diss sieve thought wizen knot tin naff—fit wizen knot tin nuff tube hack hum Oman—hid eyed don thick wrasse two's hoe thought grate hurl hove, end hid hide four ewe end four mien four thought lap pear rand four thought manned eyeing off fun gore rand thought nay kid purse son lie hung inn this treat knot own lea off cull cutter, bat off faff rick her, rand knew Yorick, kind land on, end owes slow—wand inns hiss Ted thought weal hove wan inn other ass heal hoves hitch wan no vice.

End weir reed thought tin thug has pal ferric leer lea—luff faze eye hovel hove Jew—ass isle hove ewe—ass though feather hassle hove dummy, isle hove ewe—end though ardor thee feather luffed hymn, though feather luffed hymn, me gay vim two huss, endow match will hove wan in other, wee, two, mast gyve vetch chow their runt hill lit her toss. Utters snot tea naff four ass two's hay: aisle hove gourd, bat eyed who knot luff mine neigh bear. Sent jaw inns haze sure all eye are riff ewes hay Yule hove gourd, dinned Jew dough ant luff yore neigh bore.

Hawk kin Yule hove gourd doom ewe dune knot sea, off ewe dune knot luff fewer neigh bare who mew sea, who mute hutch, wit who mule eve. End sew thus suss fairy imp aught ant four ass tour he all eyes thought luff, tube beet rue, haste who hart. Tit hart gee suss tool hove fuss, sit hart hymn. Mint tomb aches your weir ram member hiss grate luff fee maid hymns elf though bred offal live two sat ass fire rung her four hiss luff.

Hour run gore fur gourd, big horse weave bin Cree ate it four thought luff. Weave bin Cree ate it tin hiss some age. Weave bin Cree ate it tool hove end bee luffed, dinned thin knee hiss big home an tomb ache kit puss sable four ass tool hove viz heel hove diss. Him aches sums elf thee Hungary wan—thin ache hid wan—though hoe mill less swan—this hick wan—though wan imp risen—they'll only wan—thee Hun one Ted wan—undies haze, ewe dead hit whom he. Hungary four oral hove, vend thus suss thee younger off four pour peephole. Thus hiss thee younger thought chew wand eye mast fined, debt maybe inner rowan gnome.

Eye an ever fur get tan up port you nutty eye hid din visa tuner Rome wear thee hid doll the sold pear rents off sun sand aught hers Hugh wad jest pot thumb inner nuns tit you shin end four got tin may bee. Yawned eye when it their, rand eyes haw whin thought tome the yah defer a thing, beaut a fool thinks, bat aver eye buddy whistle hooking two wards thud whore. End eyed hid knots he ass ingle wan withies mile lawn there fey. Sand eye tern add two thus hiss tour rand eye ass kid: dhow wuss thought?

Howe asset thought though peephole hove a very thin ear, wire the awl hooking tow wards thud whore, wire thin knots mile ling? Eye ham sew youse two sea this mile honor peephole, leaven thud high yin once mile, lands she's head: Thus suss near lea a varied hay, there axe peck tongue, there roping thought ass Hun nerd aught her welcome viz at thumb.

There her tub big horse there four got tin, antsy—thus sis whirl havoc hums. Thought paw verity cams write their inner rowan gnome, me van egg licked tough luff. May bean hour rowan far Millie weave sum buddy hoe hiss fee lung loan lea, hoe hiss fee lungs hick, hoe hiss fee lung wherry, dinned the sword if a cult hays four a very buddy. Air wee their, air wee their tour a sieve thumb, miss thumb other their tour a sieve thatch aisled?....

.... Frame mere though jaw you've lie faff thee Hun borne chilled come sow. Tiff few big home hub earning lie tin though whirled doff piece, thin reel lea thin no bell piece pries scissor guff tough thin whore we gin peephole. Gourd Bill Hess shoe!

MUD EARN LITTER A CHEWER

Theo owe pinning oven numb air a can't Rajah day, The odd riser

Does covers hummer knight. An that all waltz off thick hummer shell art oven numb air a can sit tee-off par apse 400,000 in habit tents—hutch waltzes inn thyme hail ling her Assam ear fey bell. End hop though brads treat, know camp parrot tough lay huss shed, dull idyll Banda sicks—owe manner rub bout 50, shore, test out, wit bush a hare prod rude hing frame Hun derriere hound block fell tat, ham host Hun him port ant Luke king purr son hook harried ass maul poor table lore gone sit Chas settees, customer hilly ewe Sid byes treat pre-chew are sand sing hares.

In withy maw woo man purr raps fie veers hiss June yurt holler, knot sober rod, butt sol lid off ray mend figure us, ferry plane inn phase sand wrasse, sand jet knot tome ley, leaden wit wan and ass maul buoy hoves heaven an din Theo there Cary hing gab eye bell land sever all him bucks. Withies the rebut working in deep end ant lea bee hind, wiser gurl love if teen, nab buoy oft well fanned an no there gore love nigh on, awl fall owing a biddy ant lea, button hot two win thus eye as tickly, inn though ache off Theo theirs.

At worse sot, jet withers wheat land goor rub out tit haul. Crass sing hat rye tangles thug rate though rough heron witched hay wall kid, whiz ass heck honed can yawn lie wait red head byte wrong sand very us lions off cares switch clang doubles sand maids hutch prow grasses thumb height am mid swift lea moo Vince trims oft rough hick. Bat thole idyll grope seamed an con chose a fanny thin say of asset porpoise tomb ache it sway but wean thick intending lions oft rough hick ant pad Destry hands switch flood bye thumb.

Halving retch tannin terse action the cider this heck conned prince a pal though rough fern how quiet bear rough lie for Vinny kine, thumb an putt town thee awe gain, witch though woo man am mediate Leo pinned, sitting upper muse a crack open witch hip laced awe hide flawed him buke. Thin and din though bye billed who thumb an, sheaf hell beckon lie in withy hymn, wile thought well veer holed buoy putt townies mall camps tool inn Fran tough thee or gain. Thumb an—though faith her, ass hitch ants tubby—look tub out hymn wit seaming why dyed as your ants, sand an ounce, twit out up ear-ring took hair weather head Denny order tore sore knot.

"Wee Wilf Hurst singer him off prays, soothe hat ten aye whom hay which two hack null ledge thole horde midge onus. Well ewe hob lie jester?" Rat thus thee ell dust gurl, hoo one till know wad hat tempted two up hear has an cons schuss sand honor fact head asp pass sable, best hoed hair others limb hand Hun dove eloped fig your up pone thick amp Charon tour Ned thole heaves off though him buke, pump hing thee yaw gin why limb other robs served: "High showed thin kit mite bean ice twos hing twin ties heaven tune height—'House wheat though barm off gee sizzle hove'"

Bitc his thyme very us hum word boned din divvy jewels sieved a verse gray does sand war cuss sieve lie phone note hissing this mall grew up desse posing hits elfin thus fash Hun ness sate hated furry mow meant tow high thumb ask hance sore paws two ass certain thick car act tore off there Warwick.

The cess it antsy, cons strewed buy thumb Ann up are rental lea took on statute a tension, now ever mow bile, worse eased up awn buy hymn Mandy big Ann add dress sing thumb mass thew thae worse pacific alley hereto he rim.

Lattice awls hing twin ties heaven, thin 'House wheat though barm off gee sizzle hove'. Hat thus they hung gurl beg an twin tarp rat theme malady up Hun thee augur gnome mitten Goth in thou core acts train, gnat this aim thyme join inner wrath hair eye soap ran owe wit hat off firm other, tug heather wee there Arthur Jew be us Barrett hone off though feather.

Theo there chilled wren pipe tweak lea long, though buoy ant gurl have ink take in him bukes frame this mall piles tacked up an thee argon.

Ass this hang, these nun desk ripped end Indy fur rents treat tau dye ants gay said, hild buy though pack Yule ear it tea off sich Ann Hun import anthill hooking fame hilly pub lick lea raisin gits cull active hoise sag ants thieve fast skipped is schism end up path eye offal eye if.

Somewhere into rested dorm moo vid simper that tickly buy there Arthur Tay Mandy nadir quit fig your off thug gurl lit thee argon, owe theirs buy thee imp rack tickle land matey really inn a fish ant tacks chewer off thief farther, who swee cable hue ayes sand wrath earful abbey butt pour leak loathed fig your bees poke moor off ale your then hen knee thing gelts.

Off thug roup thumb other all hone stud outers halving thought farce sand eat termination witch, haw wave herbal lined door Erin knee us, may kiss force elf press serve ace shun, Niven hots access sin live.

Thole aster theme owe he cans, Jay fen a more coup pear

Hone thought date whom hen whirl ling a ring gone though ban kiss hove ass mall butt trap heads trim, with inn Ann ours jar nay off thee hen camp meant off web, lie hick though sewer weighted thee up ear ants oven apse scent purse on, ore thee up roach off sum axe peck Teddy vent.

They've asset can a pea off would sprayed its elf two thumb Marge in off there reaver, rover rang in thew otter, rand shad a wing gits Doric cur ant withered heap hair Hugh.

There hays off this Hun wear big inning tug growl lass fears, anther intends seat tough thud hay worse lesson daze thick hula vipers off this preens sand fount hains rosy buff there lea fib heads, end dressed tad inn thee hat moss fear.

Stealth hat brie things high lance, switch mar cuss thud row seasalt rain ass oven ham airy canal hence cape pinch Yule eye, perve aided this occlude deeds pot, tint erupted hone lea buy they'll love ices off thumb hen, Theo Cajun Alan lay zit hap over would pucker, they'd as cord ant crave sum Gordie J., auras well ling honor near, frame though duller whore river dust aunt what her full.

This fee ball land bro' Ken's hounds swear, owe waver, two family are toothy four rest hers two drawer there rat tension frame thumb whore into resting matte rough third higher log.

Wile won off the sloid terrors shod there heads kin end while duck hoot trim meant sofa neigh tiff off thew hoods, Theo the wrecks sybbe Ted, threw thumb ask off hiss rood end near lease avid Jack whip mince, though pry tour, those Hun burnet handle hung fist camp lection off won whom mite clay am diss scent frame may ewe rope Ian par rent age.

Though form ear wuss heated an thinned over Masai logan up hose chewer thought perm it Ted hymn too whiten thee affects off hiss ear nestle hang wedge, buy though gambit axe press have jest sure seven end Ian in gauged inn dab hate. Hiss buddy, witch worse sneer lien nay kid, prose ant head hatter Riff hick hem blame offed edh, drone inn inn term ingled cull hair off why ten blague.

Hassock loose leash hay vid dead, awn witch know wither hearth an though woolen own ant shiver louse calping toughed worse pray served, worse with out tournament off Fanny caned, withy axe sept shun offers holy tarry father, though crust hiss scrow nun deep ended Dover easel eft shoal door.

Rat Tommy hawk hence calp ping naïf, off ingle ash man knew facture, wear inners gird ill, why lush ought mill eat tarry rye full, off thoughts aught wit witch thee pall lacy off though Wyatts harmed theirs have edge alleys, lake hairless lea cross hiss barrens in Hughie nee. Thee axe pandered chess tough fool for middle hymns, engrave count an ants off thus war rear, wooden note though teed retched though figure offer stays, tho' nose hymn tums oft a cape eared two wave yeah tweak Anders men hoot.

Thin or thumb Eric can war rear coursed though air tubby plaqued fro mass hole buddy, ass mall toughed worse lift hone thick rowan offers said, inn odder thought hiss enema mite have ale hymns elf off fit, inner hen shin cough this calp inn thee eve vent offers foal. This calp wuss thee own lea had miss sable trow fear evict Tory.

Tusset whiz dimmed mow rim port ant two hub taint this calp then took hill thumb Han. Sum try bus sleigh rates wrasse Hun Theo knur off stray king add head buddy. This poor actor hisses save knee early dizzy peered hum mong thin deans off thee at lawn ticks Tate's.

Thee affray move thew height mange add gin buys hutch pert suss wear knot can't sealed buy husk loathes, wuss lick thought off wan hoo wad none haired sheep sand axe hair shun framers earl east you. Thus parson, tho' musk Yule are, wuss wrath air hat ten you ate head then fool, butt ever inner vend muss hill up-eared strung end dinned you rated bine remitted axe poseur ant oil.

Hue whore a Hun tin short off ore rest grin, Anders hummer capers kins switched bench horn off there fir.

Heel sew bodhran nigh Finney gird love wham pummel Ike thought twitch can fined these can Teague arm mince off though wind dean, batten know Tommy hawk.

Hiss smock ass sins wear ore numb meant head dafter though gae fash shuns off thee own leap artifice sundered wrasse switch up-eared billow thee hang hing fro quizzer pear off bucks kin laggings, thought lay stet those hides, sandwich wear gart her dub of thin niece, wither sin use over dear. Up ouch end dawn comb pleated is spare zonal lack hoot rim ants, tho' are eyeful off grate leng tho' witched a the hoary off thumb moron genius Wight sad tort thumb whiz thumb host deign jar us offal fire harms, lien dig hence din nay boar rinse apple ling.

Though why off though Hun terror scow, twitch every mite bee, worse mall, quack, e'en hand wrest less, row van wile hiss poke, connive raise hider vim, massive ink west off gay more dissed rusting these hudden op roach off sum lure king enema. Knot wit standing this hymn Tom's off hobbit you'll suss piss shun, hiss count announce wizen hot hone lea with hout gyal, butt hat thumb mow meant a twitch hears sinned road used, tit worse char Judd within nicks press shun off stir dye on nest tea.

Ankle tum scab in, Harry yet bitch hearse toe

Purr haps thumb aisle dust for muff this hiss stem moves laver ease tubby scene inn those Tay tough can't hockey.

Though jenny rill pray valence off vague rick cult Ural purse shoots over quite anger a duel neigh chewer, knot rick wiring though spear eye odd dick sea sons off furry hand press sure thought tar cold foreign thaw busy ness off Morse other in diss tricks, Mick's thought ask off thin eager owe wham whore hell the full land Reese son nibble won.

Wile thumb aster, can tent wither morgue red duels tiler Vic quiz is shun, hose knot though stamped hay shuns toward hart Edna's switch all ways sowf or come fray lieu man hate sure whin though prospective sodden ant rapper'd gainers way din though ball lance, wit know we've your count a poise then though in tressed off though hell place sand Hun pro tack Ted.

Hoe a verve as its hum mast hates their, an twit Nessie's thug hood whom erred dinned all gents have sum asters sand miss tresses, sand Theo faction ate loyal tee off sums laves, mite beat hemp Ted chewed ream thee oft fey belled poet tickle edge end over patter eye arch Alan stay chew shun, handle thought; butt aver randy bovid those seen their brewed saw port anxious shade owe—this shade owe offal haw.

Sole hungers thole hawk on Sid hearse awl thee shoe men beans, swathe bee tin carts sandal live in gay factions, hone lee ass sew money thinks bill longing two-arm aster, sole hungers though fey lure, oar miss four tune, nor imp rue dense, soared eth off thick hind a stone Norm make oars thumb many date who axe change awl lie folk hind Prot action an dene dull gents four won off hoe plus miss array ant oil, soul hung git his imp hoss able tomb ache Kenneth hing beauty fuller desire rubble inn though Bess trek you late head add minister hay shun off sleigh very.

Moustache hell bee whiz affair kinder mango wooden hate chaired end kine dully, Anders posed tweezy end dull gents oft hose a rowan dim, anther hidden ever bean alack owe Fanny thin witch mite can't rib Ute toothy fizzy cull come fort off thin knee grows honors a state. Head, dhow waver, speck you late addle lard jelly an quiet Lew's lea; hidden vole Vadim sylph dip ply, Anders snow Tess tool Argy mounted cumin toothy Hans off hay lea; an thus mall piss off infirm hay shuns thick quay tooth après ceding conifer say shun.

No wit tad sew whap end thought, tin up roach chin thud whore, eel eyes her had court ten huff off though converse hay shun tune oath hatter tray door whiz may king off first who harm aster force hum baddie. Shoe wood glade leaves topped hat thud whore tool hiss in, ash hick aim hout; butter missed tress joust think hauling, shoe as hobble eye Judd two hay sinner weigh.

Steel sheathe ought shoe herd thought raider may kin off fur four herb buoy; cutch Hebe miss taken? Hair arts welled anther hob dance shin voluntary lease trained dumbs hoe tite thought though lit all fell loll hooked tap inn tour phase inner stun ash mint.

"Eel eyes sag hurl, wart tails shooter daze?" header mist tress, wan eel eyes sad hop set thew ash-pitch her, gnaw cud town though erks tanned, dinned fie Nelly worse abs tract head lea off far ring harm missed trestle lung knight Gowan inn plaice off this ilk dray shoed hoard haired hurt tube ring frame thaw word robe.

Eel eyes are star Ted. "Owe misses!" shoes head, ray singing hair ice; thin, burr sting entered here, shoes hat dine honor share, rand big hands hob Bing. "While eyes arch isled, wore tails yews?" head harm mist tress "Ohm is as misses," head Eel eyes sir, "thaws beano tray dirt hawking wither mass stir inn though par lore! Eye haired hum." "Welts hill itch aisle, sup hose their is."

"Owe messes, dews oppose mass are woods hell ma hairy?" anther perk richer three worse elf inn two itch hair rinse hobbed can vole sieve lea.

"Cell limb! Know ewe fool ash gurl! Yew no yaw mast heron ever dills widows hath earned raiders, sand Nev ear mince two cellar knee off hiss serve ants, ass lung ass day bee have whale."

Lit all wee men, chap turf oar, Louis Sam hay all caught

Beth whist tube ash full tug hoe tusk cool. Eat tad bent ride, batch he's offered some hutch the tit whisk even op, pan shed hid hurl essence a tome wither farther.

Heave in wen hew enter weigh, Andy's mutter whisk hold tad a vote hearse kill land an edgy two sold your Sade sews eye a tees, Beth want faith flea yawn bye hearse elf fanned deed thaw Bess shake hood.

Show Izzy how's why flea lid dell Cree chewer, rand help tanner key poem nee tank home fort able further war curs, Nev hearth inking oven nay raw ward butt tube Bill avid.

Lung, quite daze schuss pent, knot lone lino Rydale, four hurl idyll whirled wasp peep holed wit hum Madge an air if rends, sand shoe wisp eye nay chewer rub Izzy be.

Their wear sick stalls tube beat ache in append rest a very moaning, four Beth wars itch aisled steal land loft harp hits a swell a sever. Knot wan hole ore and someone a mong thumb, awl wear rout caste still Beth tuck thumb inn, four wen hearse is terse sout grue the sidles, the aye past two herb a cause Amy wood hove no thin gold a rug lay. Beth chair rushed thumb mall thumb whore ten dilly four thought ferry rhea son, onset upper huss spittle foreign firmed awls.

Nope in swear heifers tuck inn two there cot tun vie tills, know arrish wards orb lows wear river give anthem, noon nag lek ta verse had end though art tough thumb host rip all sieve, bottle wharf head ink loathed, Norse stand car assed wither no faction which Nev are fayled.

Wan four lorn frag meant off dull linnet tea add be longed two Jo wand, have ingle lead at tempest shoe us lie if, whistle leftie reckan there hag beg, frame witch dree reap whorehouse sit worse risk queued buy Beth end takin tour ref huge.

A vein note hop twits said, sheet hied don earn eat lit hulk hap, pandas boat harm sandal eggs swear gon, Shea heed thee stiff fish in seas bi-fold ingot inner blank it Andy voting herb hest bade tooth hiss craw nick inn valid.

A fanny won add known thick Earl ave shed awn thought holly, eye thin kit wood haft hutched there arts, eve in wile they'll aft.

Shoe braw tit beets hove book quays, shoe red twit, two kit tout tube wreath fray share, ridden Ander hark oat, shoes hang at lull a byes hand-on ever when tube head with ow't key sing gits sturdy phase sand wisp a ring tend early "Eye hoe pule a vague hood nigh, tum eye pore deer."

Beth add dirt rubbles a swell ass Theo there, sand knot bean Ann hain gel butter ferry hue man lit hole gurl, shoe oft ten whipped till idyll wee pass Jo's head, big horse shake who dent hake mew sick less sons sand aver foin peon no.

Shell hove dumb you sick sewed ear lee, trite sew ward tool earn, ant practice tow way soap patient lee hat though gin glen olden strew meant, though tit deeds seam massive sum wan (knot twin tan tum arch) aught towel purr.

Know biddy deed, a waver, rand gnaw buddies awe Beth why pith at ears oft thee hello quays, thought wood dent quay pinch hoon, winch he wassail lone. Shoes hang lie cull idyll ark a bout hair walk, worsen ever toot hired form Army an thug earls, sand hay aft hard haze head hoop flute worse elf "Eye no while git mime you sick sum thyme, miff eye ham gude." Their arm any Beth's sin thaw hurled, shined quite, sit hing ink horn airs still knee did, handle live hing four udders sew chair fully thought know won seize this hack riff ices tilth lid dull crick eat on though earth steps chair ping, anthers wheats, hunch shy knee presents van ashes, sleeve Vince high lint sand Shah dough bee hind.

Thud Hubble deal her, Willy am conger eve

Tilth hen, suck cess swill at tend miff four win eye meat chew, eye meat thee own lea yobs tickle tomb eye four tune. Sin the yawl, lit they beaut Teague gilled mike rhymes, sand whit sew ever Ike hum it oft wretch cherry ore Dee seat, shell beam pew Ted tomb he ass sum ere rat. Wretch cherry? Water wretch cherry?

Luff can sell Saul though bands off rend ship, onsets menhir rite up on there fur stuff hound hay shuns.

Due tit oak hing, spy at hate two pair rents, graw tit chewed tube any factors, sand Fidel it hay tough rends, aired if rent ant part tick you'll art eyes. Butt than aim offer rye vole cut sum mall ass under, Andes age jenny rill lack wit hence.

Rye valley sequel, handle hove liked edh than you never sale level leer off mink hind. Habit hiss their knot Satch oath hing ass on a sty? Yea's sand whose hoe aver haze zit a bout hymn, bare sin any mien hiss Brest.

Foray whore on nest manners height hake kitties thought nigh, scrap you louse, cons see anxious purse son, hoo welsh heat know buddy bottoms elf, sot chin other cocks scum assure why's moan, hoo whist hoo heard four roll though whirled, hand twill beam aid off full off bine owe buddy butt hymns elf; ha-ha Harwell four whist home mend on nasty gif meek Hun ink hand hip okra say; Otis Satch up leisure twang ill four fare phased fuels!

Thin thought tongue rugged junk red Yule a tea well buy tat tinny thin. While atom mace sea, eye huff this aim phase, this aim wards sand hack cents wen ice peak wit eyed dew thin canned wen eyes peak wit eyed dune knot the ink, though ferries aim; end eared ass Himalayas shun hiss thee own lea heart knot tube beano win frame neigh chewer.

Wye well manic kind beef full sand beady sieved,
In wire France sandal hovers owe thus bee leaved,
Wen eat, chew surges thicket lea hiss Owen mined,
Maize hoe match frau dinned poor off baize ness fined?

Thumb meddle: ass hat hire hug hents addition, Jaw wand ride den.

Off awl or rant hicks heights sand pad gent rye
Witch ingle ash id yachts ran ink roads Tess he,
Though pole ash meddle bares though pries salon;
Amman stir, moor though favor ate off that own
The neither farce whore the ate hers hove shorn.
Ever dead heart sew hell wit nay chewer wrist arrive
Nore haver eye doll seamed some hutch all hive;

Soul hike thumb manse sew goal dint who this height,
Sew bay Swithin, sew count her feet hand late.
Ones hide ass field wit height all land wit phase,
Handle less ticking showed wan tar eagle plays,
Son there averse sat our that owns her vase,
Ore witch hour mountains honeys be hymns diss plays.
Thew horde, pronoun stall loud buy shrive elf hoise,
Lay oat a moor, witch chin po lush hiss ridge hoise,
Thud dame, mun the, your, tooth hug rate tact urge hoi Ned,
Dander knew can't ting golly day Dee signed.
Fife daze hiss ate it fur a very caste onlook,
Form whore daze thing hod two fin ash shad am tuck.
Bat toucan tail wit a sense sane gels ar
Roar howl hung have in worse may king loo cipher?
Oak hood this tile thought cope pee devour rug race
Sand pleugh wed sich far rows foreign you nick phase,
Cud hit affirmed hiss sever-chain gin wheel,

They vary us peas add hired thug raver's kill!
Am marshal leer oaf Hurst, wither leak herb
Loan, lie cup pig me, buy thew hinds, tow wore;
Hub bird list sheaf, Arab Bel-air Amman,
Soy hung hiss hate rid two wisp rinse big Ann.
Necks thus (Howe aisled lea Will ham bush shuns tear!)
Have ermine rig ling inn though use sir pears sear,
Bar tarring hiss vein awl whit force hums off goaled,
Hick as Tim's elfin tooth assent lyke mauled;

Grown Ned, side, hand preyed, wile coddle in ness whisk hain,
Thole how dust beg-pie puff this quick king trayne.
Butt asters ard touch heater jug glare sighs,
Hiss sew pennal you'd Ness hick hood neared ask eyes.
Theirs pleat this ain't; four rip a critics heel
A louse snows in butt though sit Cancun seal.

Whoa ring tusk candle gave stool lar jazz copes;
Ain't sum mussed knot raid, both Aimee antelope.
Thee an god lea prints apple wassail this aim,
Butter grows chit bitter haze hiss part nurse came.
Bees hides, there pays whores for mill, grey Vance ends lack;
Hiss in hymn ball whit tout ran thee have eye peck.
Yachts till hoof hound hiss fort unit ass Tay,
Hold roves off blow kids chock king upper sway;
They'd hook, butt knot raw war did, hiss add vice;
Fill in hand whit axe actor dub ill pries.
Poor whizzes same; both rowan frame thought prate hence,
Tho' retch tarn Ned low yell inner sewn duff fence,
Sand mall is recon sigh all dim two hasp rinse.
Hymn mean thee hang witch offers whole hiss surfed,
Raw hoarded fuss stirs till thin need is surfed.

Bee hold dim know axe halted din toot rust,
Hiss consoles soft convene ants, held dome juice,
Stephen inn thumb host sins seared vice hie gay
Via dug rudd gins till Toby in nave.
Tough rods hill earn tin is fan attic yours
May dim an easy inners low flog years.
Sat Bess tassel idyll on nest ass hick hood,
Unlike why twitches, miss Chivas leg hood.
Two hiss forced buyers long ingle lea heal e'en
Sand wrath her wood big rate buy wick head miens.
This fray mud fir rill, heel loos dour trip pill old,
(Had vice sun safe, press up at us, sand bowled.)

Hat hat lore assay yawns pear thyme, Joe's if Adders on

Wee awl off fuss camp lane off thus shore tin ness oft thyme, say this any candy ate huff match mower thin wean know hot ado wither lie vis has here's pent eye there undoing know thin gat haul, ore undoing know thin toothy porpoise, ore undoing know thin thought wee otter due. Weir awl ways camp lane inner dais ore phew, wand hacked hing ass thou their woodbine hoe wend off thumb. Thought know bull fill loss suffer desk cry bid dour ink hone cyst hence sea withers elves sin thus part tick yew lar, buy haul though sever eye us terns off axe press shun end that's switch ore peck you liar two hiss right hing.

Sigh off ten cons hid door monk hind ass holy ink on cyst tent wit hits elf inn up hoy ant thought bares hum off fin at he toothy for mere. Thou wheeze seam gree vedette this aught ness off lie fin gen aural, weir whish hing ever hip eerie hod off fit hat tin hend. Thumb miner lungs Toby a phage, thin two beam an off bus ness, thin tomb ache a pan nest hate, thin two are hive a ton hers, thin two rat hire. Thistle though thee hole love lie fizzle loud buy aver rye won Toby shore it, these aver ill divvy shuns off fit up ear lung ant hideous.

Wear furl ankh thinning ours pan hinge jenny rill, butt wood feign can't racked though parrots off witch at his camp hosed. Thee you surer wood beaver eye waltz hat is fie do avail though thyme a nil he yea Ted thought lice bat wean though press ant mow meant tanned necks quart heard hay.

Thee pulley tush in wood bee can tented tool ooze tree ears sinners sly if cud hip lace thin goes in though pose stewer wit chief fan sees thee wall Stan din aft hers hutch are revel you shun off thyme. They'll hover wood big lad toast rye cow tough hiss axe is tense awl thumb owe mince the tart hoop ass a weigh bee four thee hap pie meat hing. This is fist ass hour thyme runes swish hood beaver eagle lad, inmost par tough hurl hives, though tit wren mush fuss stir thin net dose.

Sever allure off thud hay hang-up honor rands, neigh, wee wash owe hay holy ears; ant ravel threw thyme mass threw whack hunt try tref hilled wit money while led hand hem tea waists, switch wee wood feign Harry hover, the twee mayor hive vat though sever awl idyll set all mint sore am magi nor eye pints off wrest twitch hard ass pursed opened own a knit.

Off weed do vied they'll lie faff must Menin toot when type arts, wish hall fined thought hat list nigh on teen off thumb arm ear gap sand Cass sums, switcher nigh there felled wit play sure gnaw busy ness. Eyed who knot, a waver, ink lieu din disk all cull hay shun though lie foe though semen whore inner perp pet you all Harry offer fairs, butt off though zone alley whore knot tall ways in gauged inn sins affection; end eye hoe pie shell knot dew wan nun hacks apt table peas huff serve ace tooth ease purse sins, a fie pint tout tooth hems her tin me thuds forth off hill ling hop there hemp teas paces off live. Thumb math hods ice shell prop hose tooth hem arrows fall low.

They'll ache eye love Inners free, Dub all ewe bee hates

Eye Willy rye sand gown how, wand goat who win as free,
A nigh in bin rose swill eye hove their, ah eye forth thee Hun nib he,
Handle liver loan inn thee be aloud gleyed.
Hand eye shell loves home piece their, four piece combs draw pings low,
Draw ping frame they've ails off them awning two hair thick rickets hings;
Their midden knights awl lag limb her, rand none up her pull glue,
Wand even nine fuller thug Lynn net swings.
Eye Willy rye sand gone how, four awl ways nigh tinned hay
Eye earl ache what her lap hing withal owes hounds buy this sure;
Wile eyes tanned don there rowed weigh, yore Ron thee pave mince Graeae,
High ear written thud heap art score.

Rid beige off cur ridges tea van crayon

Their whiz aye you though full pry vat tool hiss end wit Teague her rears toothy wards off that all sold you're unto thief air ride commence off hiss come raids. Aft are a sieving off hill off dick cushions sconce earning march as hand at hacks, hew wen two whiz Hutton craw willed threw wan inn trick hate howl thoughts her vid hit ass adore. Hew witched tube bee all hone wits home knew that's thought addle ate leak hum toe hymn.

Hill aid own none awe hide bank thoughts tret Chad a cross though rheum. Inn Theo there rend, crack herb ox is swarm aid two sir vis fern a chewer. The hay war groped hub out thee fie ore plaice. Up picked chewer fro' men ill youse tray Ted weak lea whiz up on they'll hog waltz, sand tree rye fills warp arrow lulled don pigs. Egg whip mints sung awn hand dip row Jack shuns, handsome tinned hashes sleigh up honors mall pie love fire would.

Off hold dead hint whiz air Venus are hoof. This Hun light, with out, beet Inga punnet, maid hit glower lie cello Shea. Dismal wind owes show tan able leaks queer off why tirl height up on thick clattered flower. This moke frame though fie rat thymes niggle acted thick lay shim neigh hand dree thud in tooth a rheum, anthers full hymn see shim neigh hock lay in Styx may dinned less there ate stew setter blaze thee hole lest stable ash mint.

They ewe the wuss inner lit all trant suffer stun ash mint. Sew the war hat lost go wing tough height. Tun thumb arrow, pair apse, their wood beer bottle, land hew wood bean knit. Foray thyme me worse hop lie Jed tool hay bear tomb ache hymns elf bee leave. Hick hood knot except wee this your rants a gnomon thought tea whiz a bout tomb ingle inn wan off thus grey tough airs off thee air. Thee head, off cursed, reamed off bat tools hollers live—off Fagin double lad dick Hun flicks thought add thrill dim withers weep end fiere. Envies yawns see add scene hymns elf fin men eyes trug ills. See Adam Madge end peepholes a cure inn though shad owes suffers sea goal lied prow hiss. Spatter wake key add rig hard dead Bat ills ask rim sun blow chizz sun thee pay jazz off though passed.

Head putt thumb mass thinks off though buy gone withers thou Tim mages off have Vic rowans sand Cass holes. Their whiz apportion off thew hurled sister eye witch head rig guarded ass that thyme off wore spat tit, heath ought, tad bin lone gun owe veer thee whore eyes on end dad diss up eared four river. frame mess hoe miss ewe with fool ice saddle hooked up on thew whore inner sewn can tree wit his trussed. Tit mast bee sums aught offer player fare. Head lunged a spare dove wit ness in gag reek likes trug gulls. Hutch wood bee gnome hoar, heads head. Man wear bet her, arm whore Tim hid. Sack you lair hand-drill aegis said you cay shun hid off faced thee throw tug rappelling inn stank, tore rills fir rim fine ants celled inch heck though pass shins.

Head burr Ned's ever all thymes twin list. Tails off grade move mints shuck they'll hand. The aim mite knot bead ass tin cud lea home Eric, butt their seamed two beam hutch glow rhea inn thumb. Head red off mar chess, aegis, cone flicked, sand head lawn good two seat awl. Hiss buzz eye mined hid rowan four hymn larch pecked yours sexed raw Vegan tin cull her, Lou rid wit breath list heeds.

Butter smother hid ass courage dim. Shed duff acted tool hook wit sum can't temped up awn thick Wally tee-off hiss warder rand pat riot his sum. Sheik hood cam lease eat terse elf fanned wit know a parent tiff faculty gave hum any hand reds offer ease suns way hew worse off vest lemur imp Hortence son though firm then awn though feel doff bat hole. Shed dads hurt in weighs off hacks press shin thought hold dim thought hearse state mints son this object cam frame mad heap convict shin. Mow rover, honors hide, whiz hiss bee leaf the Torah thick hill mote heaven thee ague mint whiz imp prig noble.

Atlas tow ever, head maid form rib bell eye on nag gains thus shell owl height thraw Nippon thick collar rough fizz ambush shins. Thin knew spay purrs, though gas sip off though fill edge, jazz sown pick touring sad are housed hymn tuan hunch heck Hubble dig rhea. Thee wore untruth fie ting fie in lead own their. All must ever raid hay thin hews pay purr preen Ted dick counts offered a sigh sieve hick Tory.

Wan height, ass heel hay inn bade, though wince sad curried two hymn thick languor ring guff thee chew arch bellows omen thus eye assed jar cud their hope for antic alley toot hell that whist had noose suffer grate bat hole. These vice off though peep hole ridge icing inn thin height hid maid dim shiv herring up roll-on gad deck stay see off hicks height mint. Lay tore, head gunned own twee smothers rheum man dads poke in this: "Maim go wing twin list."

Inn west minister rabbi, jay bet shaman

Lit meat hake thus owe thug love of,
Ass though fox Hugh man as well,
Sand though beauty us fills off feed hen
Basque bin heath he yabbie belle.
Seer, wearing lands stay Timon lisle
Hiss into allay desk rye.
Grace yes lured, dough bum thatch Herman's,
Pear there wee men fourth eyes hake,
Hand off thought hiss knot who wheezy
Wee wall par done thumb ass take.
Bat grace yes lore, twat ears shell bee,
Done to litany wan bum he.
Quay poor hemp hire run diss ma'am bird
Guy dour four says buy they and,
Gall ant bell axe frame forge ham ache ha,
Hand your ass sand tow goal hand;
Prow tacked thumb laud din awl there fie it,
Sandy van mower prow tacked though heights.
Thin cuff water neigh shin stance four,
Bukes frame beauts hank Hun trill hains,
Freeze peach, if reap asses, claws dust ink shin,
Dim hock racy end prop herd rains,
Laud, putt bin Neath eyes pish auk hair
Wan hay tea nigh nick a dog'gones queer.
All tho' deer laud eye ham ass inner,
Eye hove dun gnome age auk rhyme;
No aisle comb two even answer vice
Wince sew waver eye huff thought thyme
Soul laud wrasse serve form he ache rowan,
Hand dew notelet mice shears goad own.
Eye wee lay bore fourth eye kin dumb,
Hell purl had stew in though hoar,
Sinned why tough heathers too thick Howards,
Joy in thew omens arm ache whore,
Thin watch this tips are hound thigh throw-in
Inn thee at earn all save tease hone.

Know eye fee loll idyll batter,
Wore tit rhea two ear thigh ward,
Wear though Bowen's off flee dins stay 'tis mean
Nave sew oft hen bean in turd
Hand know, deer laud, eye can knot weight
Big horse eye hovel launch honed ate.

Hub bear lend ire rhea, Kris two four Esher would

Frame high wind owe, thud heaps all hymn ass hives treats. Hell arch hops wear thole amp spurn awl deign dearth hush had owe oft hop bevy ball cone eyed face adds, dare tip last her frowned edges some bussed wits crow all wore canned her old dick dove ices. Thew holed is tricked tussle hike thus: treat lea din inn twos treat off how says sly Kush abbey man you meant hall say fuss scram mid withy tarn hushed valley you able sand sick honed and fern a chewer offer bank rapt mid dull claws.

Eye yammer cam error withy hit shatter rope ink, white pass sieve, rack hoarding, knot thin king. Rack hoarding thumb an Che vin gat thew in dough oppose it an though woo man inn thick a mow know ashen nor hare. Summed hay, yawl the swill huff two bead of eloped, kerf alley preen Ted, feck Sid.

A Tate tock lock-in though weave inning though hawse dour swill bill hocked. Thatch hill drainer halving sapper. Thee all lector rick sigh ness witch don know veer thin height belle off they'll idyll low talon thick horn air, wear Yukon higher are rum bye thee our. Ensue in thew hiss ling wheel big inn. Yang manner culling there gurls. Tanned inn dawn therein thick hold, thew wassail a pat though lie Ted wind hoes off worm rheum's worth abed sore all red die tern do in four thin height. The wan tube bee lit inn. There's hick nulls heck hoed own thud dip poll lost treat, lass civvy us sand pry vet hands had. Big horse off thew is sling, eye dune hot cart whose Tay hear inn thee heave nuns. Sitter a mind Smith hat time inner fur rains hit teal hone fur frame ohm.

Sum thyme sigh weld at ermine knot tool hiss hint who wit, peek open buke, trite whore heed. Bat sue nick hall assure twos hounds owe peer sings hoe wins cyst tents hoed a spare ring lea you man, thought atlas tie half tug het opened pee up threw this lats off they've a niche humble hind tomb ache quiet shore the tit a snot—ass eye no fairy wallet cud knot posse Billy bee—form he.

Ticks tree ordain Harry's melon thus rheum win this tow vessel height a Dan thew in dowers shot; knot awl tug heather run please ant, tum Mick's stew rove inn sense sands tale bunce. Thought halt aisled stow of, gorge as leak hollered, lie can alter.

Thew ashes tanned Laika go thick share rein. Thick Hubbard awl sewers go thick, wit car vid Cath heed roll win doughs: buzz marque fey says thick Inga press ear inn stay end gloss. May bust share wood doofer rub bee shops thrown. Inn thick horn earth rhea shame midday evil hull birds (frame math he a trick ill Turing camp any?) ore fuss tend tug gather two for ma hats tanned. Frills showed herons crews thee Hades off tree hail birds sand Polish has thumb frame thyme two thyme. There have hay end shore pen huff took ill.

A very thin gin there rumors lick thought; ton ness ass airily so lid, Abner maul lie heave viand Dane jar us leas harp.

Pea tarp an, Jay ham bar ray

Though buoys van a shin inn thug loom, inn dafter up haws, butt knot ill hung paws, forth hing scow brusque Leon though eye land, comb though pyre ate son third rack. Wee ear thumb bee forth hay arse sin, hand titters awl ways this aimed red fills hung:

"Of vast bill hay, oh hoe, hive two, up irate hing wig ho,

End off wire poor Ted buyers show, twills your tomb meat bill low!"

Am whore villa ness Lou king lotah nave a rung inner rowan exec you shin duck. He rail idyll inn add vans, sever end a gain withies said tooth thug roundel is hen ninnies gray tar miss bear, pea says off fate inner seers is horn numb hints, his though and summit alley an Czech owe, hook hut is nay men let hers off blowed don though beck off though Gavin her off though prise on hat gay owe. Thought jig antic Blake bee hind dim his sad men neon aims sins hid wrapped thee wan wit witch do skim others till terra fie thatch ill drain hone though ban cuss off thug wad you mow.

Hear as bilge hooks, a very in chuff hymn tat hood, this aim bilge hooks hug hot sicks does anon thew all Russ frame Flynn tub a foray wood rope though beg off my doors (Port chug geese goaled peace his); sand cook sums head tub bee bull lack more fizz broth hair (butt these wizen ever proofed), an gin till manse tar key, wants in hush sure inner po blacks cool lands tilled ain't he inn hiss sways off culling, hence Kyle heights (morgue inns Kyle heights); hand though eye rush bow sons me, a nod ledge genie all moan whose tabbed sew twos peak, with how tough fence, sand whiz Theo Nelly nun can form mist inn nook screw, wand new dull her, who sands wharf hexed don beck words, sand robot mull hence sand elf may soon end men knee Ann other rough fennel lung no-one hand fired awn this pan ash mane.

Inn thumb mist tough thumb, though Blake kissed tanned lore jest inn thought ark sitting, rick lined jay muss who chorus hire oat hymns elf, jazz who cough who mitt as head Dee whiz Theo win lemon thought this Hickock fee red.

Heel hay hatters seize inner off char riot drone end prop hell lid buy hiss Menin dins Ted offer rite Tandy add thee eye run nook wit witch haver hand an on hie yen cur raged thumb twin crease there pays. Ass dugs thus terra bill mint tree Ted undid dressed thumb, Anders dugs Theo bayed hymn. Inn purse on hew whisk add aver us (stead luck in) end bill lack of eyes (dare cough aced), Andy's hare whizzed wrest inn lung corals, switch hat ill idyll dissed tense lucked lie cob lack handles, sand gay vis sing you lar lithe retaining axe press shin two hiss hands home count in hence. He sighs wear off though blew off though four get mien hot, end offer proof hound melon collies, have wen hew wasp lunging hassock enter ewe, a twitched I'm tour heads pots up eared din thumb handle it tap whore ably.

Inn manors, sum thin guff though grounds in yours till clang two hymn, sew thought tea Eve inner hipped chew whip within errand eye hove bent holed thou tea whiz are rack on tours (Tory tell her) rough rip Ute. Hay worsen ever mowers in a stir thin wen hew ass must pole light, twitches prow bubbly that rue whist Tess tough breading, an thee hell leg ants off hiss dick shun, Niven wen hie whiz wearing, know Les thin thee dissed stink shin off hiss dim mean our, shod dim wan offer defer ink hast frame hassock rue.

Ham manner vend omit table carriage, hit worse head thought Theo in lea thin geese hide hat whiz this height off hiss sewn plod, witch whiz thicken doff in anew sue whelk holler. Undress seize hum what taped thee at hire ass owe see hated wit thin aim off char Liz too, halving herd its head inn sum earl ear peer aye odd offer scare rear though tub whore assed ranger assemble ants toothy elf hated stew arts; sand inners mow thee adder roll dour off hiss sewn can't rye vans switch unable dim twos moke too sag arse sat ones. Button dough tidally thug rim must par tough hymn whiz hiss eye rank law.

Laugh fill ear cape pea Angie, Tea ass sell yacht

Stan Don though eye hissed pave mint tough this tears,
Lea nun agar din earn,
We've, we've this Hun lie tin yore air,
Class pure flours two ewe wither paned sour prize,
Filling thumb toothy grind intern
Wither few jet of recent mint tenure ice:
Butt we've, we've this Hun lie tin yore air

Sew eye wood hove Adam live
Sew eye wood hove adders tanned ant grieve,
Sew we wood hove lift
Ass this hole lives though buddy toe run end brew Sid
Ass thumb hind asserts though buddy eat hiss you Sid.
Ice shoed fined
Sum weigh ink hum parable lea lie tend eft.
Sum weigh web oath shoed danders tanned
Seem pill land fey the less has arse mile land Shea cuff thee and
Sheet earned a way, butt withy aught hum whether
Camp held mime Madge in nation men need hays,
Men need hays sand men knee ours:
Hair hare rover hair alms sand hair alms fuller flours.
Sand eye wander row this shoed hove bean tug heather!
Eye shoed half lust tad jest you're an dope hose
Sum thymes this codger Tay shins till am maze
That rub bulled midden knight an thin nun's rip pose.

Alleys his sad ventures sin wand hurl hand, Lou whisk carol

Alley Swiss big inning tug het ferret hired duffs hitting buyers hiss tear Ron though ban can doff halving no thin to-do: wince aught wise shed pip tint tooth Hebe hookers hiss tore whiz reed hing, butt tit tad know pick chewers soar converse say shins inn at, "tanned waters though youse offer buck," though tall is "with oat pick chewers sore converse say shone?" Sushi whisk cone side ring inner rowan mined (a swell ash hick hood, forth a hut dame aid hair fill fairies leap pea hand stew pit), weather though play sure rough may king gay days each hain wood bee wore that rubble off get hing up-end pea king thud hay seas, wins sod in lea awe height raw bit wit pin Kaiser ankle hose buyer.

Their wizen know thin sew fairy rum ark Hubble inn thought; gnawed hid alleys thin kits hoe fairy mutt shout off thew hay two ear there habits hate who wits elf, "Owed ear! Owed ear! Eye shell bale hate!" (winch he thaw tit hover raft towards, sit hock curd two hair thoughts shy hot two halve one dirt hat thus, butt hat that thyme metals seamed dick white nature all); bat wen there habit hack chew all lit hooker what shout off fits waste cote pock hit, end luck tat tit, tanned thin harried don, alleys tart head two wharf eat, ferret flushed dick crosser mined thought shed Nev verb a fore sinner habit wit eye there raw waste cote pock it, Torah what chat toot hake outer fit, tanned burr nine wit curio city, sheer Annika Ross though feel dafter writ, tanned four tune it lea whiz jest inn thyme twos he hit pup dawn earl urge rob bit toll an dearth he edge.

Inn on other mow meant town win Tallis soft a written ever wince con Sid a ring Goan thew hurled shoe whiz tug het tout tug hen.

There habit toll whence trait unlike at ton nil force hum weigh, in thinned hipped sadden lead own, sew sadden lea thought alley sad knotty mow mint tooth ink hub outs topping hearse elf bee four sheaf hound hearse elf hauling downer ferried heap whale.

Eye there thaw hell whiz ferried heap, Porsche he fail ferries lowly, four shed plan tee-off thyme mash he wen town tool hooker bout heron two wander watt whisk hoeing two hop pin axed.

Firs chit ride tool hook dhow nand may cow twat shoes combing two, bat tit whist hood ark two sea yen knee thin; thin shill hooked tat this hides off though hell, land know test thought the wharf hilled wit cub hordes sand bukes shell viz; seer ran theirs he sore mops sand pick chewers sung up awn pigs. Sheet hook dough nudge are frame wan off thus shell viz ash hip assed; hit whiz lay billed 'Ore range mar malady', bat tour grate diss up point mint tit whiz amp tie; shed hid knot lick two'd wrap though jaw ear four fee rough kill ling sum bodies hoe man edged two putt tit tin two won off thick hub hordes ash sheave hell parse tit. "Will!" tho' Tallis tours elf, "aft hearse hutch off all ass thus, eyes shell thing gnaw thin cuff tum billing dunce tears! Hub rave the ill loll thin cuff meat tome! Wye, eye woo dense hay yen a thin gab out tit, eve inn iffy full laugh that hop off thee how!" (switch whiz ferrule Ike lit rue.)

Thin uke a losses, Emil as are us

Knot lick though bray singe eye ant off creek fey him,
Wit conk a ring lyms as tried frame lend who'll and;
Hear rat towers hew ash sheds, Hun sat gay Tess shells tanned
Dumb mite he womb man wither tore, choose flay
Miss thee imp risen Ned lightening, an darn aim
Other rough axe isles. frame herb beak on and
Glue swirled why dwell come, harm isled dice come manned
There breed Jed tar bear thought wins hit teas fray me.
"Key, pain shunt lends, sure store eyed pump!" cry shchi
Wits high lent tool hips. "Gyve mere tie herd, yore pure,
Yore had all dim asses year nine tubby for he,
Thew retch hid riff fuse off yurt he-men sure.
Sinned this, thee hum lest hemp pissed toast tomb he.
Isle if tomb isle amp bee sighed though goal dinned whore."

Sun knits frame thaw port you geese, All is hub bath bar at brow none

How-do aisle hove the? Lit Mick can't though hays.
Isle hove the tooth adept thinned bread than dye it
Mice hole canner retch, wen filling gout off site
Forth he yens off bee hing canned dead eyed heel grays.
Aisle hove the tooth all evil love a very dais
Mows quieten heed, buy son end can delight.
Isle hove the frilly, ass mince tri-four rite;
Aisle hove the poorly, ass that earn frump raise
I'll hove the wither pass shin putt two youse
Cinema hole dug reefs, sand wit match aisled hoods fey.
Thigh ill hove thew wither luvvies he mud tool ooze
Wit mile host Seine 'tis, aisle hove the withy burr eths,
Miles, steers, offal mile lie!—fanned, off gad chews,
Eye shell bottle hove the butter raft herd eth.

Thatch Harriet, A mill eyed hick in sun

Beck horse eye cud knots top ford eth,
Thick hind lease topped firm he;
Thick are ridge hell lid butt jesters elves
Sand dim or tall lit he.

Wheeze low lid rove, venue know waste,
Tanned eye hid putter weigh
Mile hay burr, rand mile assure two,
Forays sieve ill at hay.

Whip assed this cool wear chill drain pulley Yid,
There less son scare slid dun;
Weep assed though feels off gray sing gray in,
Wop assed this set on son.

Whip horsed bee foray howe seethe hat seamed
Is welling off though grow wand;
There hoof whiz cares lea visa bill,
Thick horn ice butter mounts.

Hints thin Tess cent your ease; bat teach
Fill shore tour thin thud hay
I've versed sir am iced though worse ass said
Swear tow word at earn a tea.

Gyve meal he Bertie ore gyve mead eth, Pat rack hen rhea

Off whey witch tube beef rhea—off whim e'en tope reserve in violet though sin nest him able privy ledges four witch wee hove bin soul hung can tenting—off wee me in hot baize lea two hub hand on thin hoe bills trug gallon witch weave bins hole longing gauged, end witch wee hove play Jed whores elves Nev air two a band on nun till thug lore yes hob jacked tough fir cone test shell bee yob Tay end—whim host fie tire up peat hits, her, whim host fie! Tan up peel two harm sand two gad off hose 'tis as Saul thought his lift huss!

The tellers, her, thought weir week; a nibble took hope wit sofa mid double lane add verse Harry. Bat wench hall wee beast rung gar? Wallet bee thin axed weak earn axed your? Wallet bee wen wear tow tally diss harmed, an winner Brit ash gourd Shelby stays shin din a very how's? Shell wig Arthur's Tring tho' buy are a solution an din action? Shell weak choir thumb inns off affect jeweler assistance bile eyeing soup pine lea honor beck sand hogging thud eel you save fanned Tom off hoe punt ill hour Rennie me shell hove binders sand on fit? Seer, wee Arnott tweak off whim ache up rapper youse off though Smee inns switch thug hod oven aitch your wrath play sedan ore poor. Thumb ill yawns off peephole, are mud inn though wholly course offal lie Bertie, an dance hutch hick Hun tree ass thought twitch weep awes Hess, Arran Vince Hubble buy hen knee farce switch hour hen hum meek consent tug gains toss. Bees hides, her, wish hell knot fie tore bottles sole lone.

The Russ edge host go dupe resides off nay shins, sand do ill ray sup fronds tough height tour bottles four ass. Though bottles, her, a snot toothy strung gallon; a test toothy vigil lent, thee act have, though breve. Bus hides, her, weave Noel action. Off wee wear baize in off two'd as hire a titties snow tool hate tour attire frame thick cone test. Their a snore a treat buttons hub miss yawn ends lay very! Owe arch answer four Jed! There clan king maybe herd awn though planes off boss tone! Thew whore risen ever table—handle late tit comb! Mire a peat tits, her, late tit comb.

Mutt a sin veins, her, two axe ten you ate thumb attar. Gen till moan Mick ripe ease, peas—butt their risen hope ease. Though worries sacked you alley big Hun!

Thin axed gay ill thoughts weeps frame thin Nore eth well hub ring tour hears thick lash offer as hound dung harms! Sour breath a wren Aral red Dionne though feel lid! Wise tanned wee hear eye dull? Waters sit thought gen till mean wash? Watt wood the hay hove? Vassal live sewed ear, are piece sews wheat, aster bee poor chaste tat though pries off chins sands lay very? Four bed hit, haul my Teague hod! Eye now knot watt coarse a theirs mate hake; bat has form he, gyve meal he Bertie ore gyve mead eth!

Gray ticks pecked tay shins, Char lust dick hens

Eye whiz burn hat blunders tone inns huff folk, corps 'they're buy', ass this hay inns cot lend. Eye whiz up host hummus chilled. Muff others sighs sad claws dap on they'll height off thus swirled sex man thus, win my know pinned owe knit. Their assume thin stray hinge tomb he, eve in know, win there affliction

Thought tin averse army; yawned sum thin stray in jar yacht tin this shew doughy ream amber rants thought eye hove ovum eye farce ditch aisled dish ass sew see hay shins withers why tug raves tone inn thatch urge shard, din dove thinned a fine Hubble camp passion eye you said two fill four idyll eyeing outer loan their inn thud harken height, twin hurl idyll poor lore whiz worm amber right wit fie rand canned ill, land thud whores suffer how swear—awl must crew alley, its seamed tomb he's hum thymes—boll Ted end lock tug hence tit.

In ant tough miff others, sand cons sequentially hug grate ant off my in, off who mice shell love mower tour a late bind buy, whiz though print supple magnet tough four fame mill hay.

Missed rot would, dormers bets hay, Esme perm other awl whisk holder, winch he's efficiently hove arc aim mired red off thus formed able purse son age tomb men shin hair rat tall (witch wassail dome), head bin mar eyed twa huss binned Jung gore thin hairs elf, hoo whiz fairy hands home, axe sipped inn this hence off though ohm lea add edge, 'hands home miss, thought hands home doze'.

Furry whiz strung lease as pecked tit tough halving be tin muss bets hay, yawned heave in off halving wants, sunny diss Pugh Ted quest shin off sup lies, maids hum hays tea butt deter manned a range mints tooth rower rout off fat who pear roughs tears win dough.

The sever dents often ink hump hat ability oft hamper rind used muss bets say toupee hymn muff, fanned if act ass sip oration buy mute you whelk hand sent. Hugh win two wind dear withies cap it all, land their, rock hoarding tour whiled ledge end inn off homily, Hugh whiz wants e'en rye din hone inn Nelly font, ink hump any wither Bob boon.

Bat eye thin kit most hove bin nab hub boo—ore rub big hum. Many howff rum end ear tied hing sufficed eth wretch tome, with inn hen yours.

Howe the off acted may ant, know buddy new; four rum media Tillie a pone this apparition, sheet hook harm aid den neigh mug hen, bore tack hot edge inner ham let awn this hick host all hung weigh a fist table ash terse elf their asses sing hull womb man wit ones her vent, end whiz Hun durst hood tool hives a clue did, diva rafter words, inner nun flecks sable retire mint.

Miff other head wants bean off favor writ off hairs, eye bull heave; bitch he whiz more tally off front head buy hiss mar rage, on thug round thought mime other whiz owe 'whacked haul'. Shed nave are sin mime other, bat shin knew hair two bean knot jet when tea.

Miff other rand miss bet sane ever meter gain. Hew whist Hubble mime other sage whinny mar raid, hand-off buttered deli Kate cone state you shin. Heed eyed aye ear raft awards, sand, ass eye hooves head, sicks man thus bee four eye Cay mint who thaw hurled.

These whiz this Tate tough mat hairs, awn thee aft or noon off, wore time hay bee axe cue Sid fork hauling, thought of vent fool land dump or tent fry day. Ike can Mick know clay I'm their four two huff no-one, hat thought thyme, home hatters stud; ore two hove hen ear rim ember rant says, found deaden thieve a dents off May own sin says, off watt fall lows.

Though there tea nigh in-steps, Jaw in buck in

Eye rat earned frame this hit tea a bout there he hock lock awn thought may oft turn noon prat tea well disk hosted wit lie. Fie hid bean there him on thus sin Theo willed can't tree, hand whiz fad dap wit tit. A fanny win head tolled mea your rug hoe thought eye wood hove bean fee lung lick thought eye shoed hovel aft tat hymn; butt their whiz though faked.

Thaw ether maid meal ever rich, that hawk off Theo word dinner eye ingle ash man-made miss hick, Ike hood dent gat tin off axe her size, sand Theo muse mints offal undone seamed diss flatters owed owe otter thought hasp peens tanned den inn though son. "Rich hard Danny", eye capped Helen mice elf, "yew hove gat tint who though runged hitch, muff rend, end Jew wad batter claim hout." Hit may dumb Hebe height mile hips tooth ink off though planes eye hid bean bulled hing gap though lost sheer sin bull away owe.

Eye hid gut may pie linnet wan off though beg wince, bat goody no firm he; yawned eye hid fig your redoubt awl kine sough weighs oven joy yin mice elf. Miff other rid braw tummy hout frame scat lend it thee yea Jove sex sand eye hidden ever bean gnomes hints; swing land whiz assort tougher hay bean heights tomb he, yawned Ike how in Ted once topping their forth arrest off may dais. Butt frame though fur sty worse diss appoint head withy hit. Tin hub bout owe weak eye whist hired duffs sea insights, sand unless thin ermine thigh added dun off offer rest you rants sand the haters in trace meat hing.

Sighed know reel palled who Gower bout wit, witch prow bubbly axe plane thinks. Plan tea off peephole envy Ted meat who there rouses, bat thud hidden seam match shin trussed Ted inn myth. Hay wood full hing mere quest shin aught tour bouts how they've rack are, rand thin gat anther rowan off airs. Zealot tough imp ear realist lay diss sass kid meat who tee tomb eats cool musters frame knew seal land ended it horse frame van cover rand thought whiz thud his molest buzz ness off fall. Hear whiz eye, there 'tis heaven yours sold, sow wind inn win din lym, wither naff moan eye two hove hug hood thyme, yaw nun may hid doff old hay.

Eye adjust hob hout set old took leer rout hang het beck toothy felt, four eye whiz though bussed board dumb an inn thee you knighted king dumb. Thought tough turn nun eye hid bean wore eying mi brow curse hub out tin vest mints tug heave mime hinds hum thin two whirr con, undone me weigh ohm mite earned inn two Mike lubber other op hothouse, switched toucan coal lone eye all mum bears.

Eye adder longed rink, canned dread thee heave nun pay purse. The wear fall off their rowan thin ear ease, tanned their wizen art tickle hob bout carol eye dies, though creek pram ear. Ire other fan seed though chop. frame maul lack counts hiss seamed though wan Begum an inn thus Shaw; wand hip laid ass trait gay meat who, witch whiz mower think hood bees head form host off thumb. Eye go third thought the ate head dim prat tub lack lie yin burr Lynn envoy Hannah, butt thought wee wear Gowan twos tick buy hymn, hand wan pay purrs head thought tea whiz Theo win lea bar rear bit wean ewe roe panned army gad don.

Eye rum member wander ring off Ike hood git edge hob inn though spurts. Sits truck myth hat all bane ear whiz this aught off plaice thought mite kip Amman frame Eyeore nun.

Whin knee though pew, Aye aye mill in

… inn witch peg lit meat sir heifer lump.

Wand hay, whin kris tow fur hob inn end whin knee though pew wand peg lit wear awl torque hint who gather, kris tow fur hob inn fin hushed them howf fool hue whiz heating inns head curl hiss lea ; “eye sour heifer lump tweed hay, peg lit.”

“Watt whiz zit dough wing? Gassed peg lit.

“Juice tall humping all long,” Sid kris tow fur hob inn. “Eyed owned thin kits home he.”

“Ice haw wan wince,” head peg lit. “Attlee sty thin cad hid,” hiss head. “Own lip air hops sit wizened.”

“Sewed hid ice,” head pew, wand daring water heifer lump whistle hike.

“Ewe done toughen seethe hems,” head kris tow fur hob ink hairless lea.

“Knot knows” head peg lit.

“Knot hat thus thyme off yours,” head pew.

Thin the yawl torque dub out sum thin gilts, sun tiller twist thyme four pew wand peg lit tug hoe hummed hoe gather. Rat fur wrist ass this tumbled all long though pa twitch hedged though wonder rid ache or would, they’d hidden same hutch two witch owe there; bat whin thick aim tooth hissed ream, ended hell put teach hath her rock cross these steppe hing stow wins, sand wear hay bell two works hide buys hide hug hen hover thee hither, the big hand toot hawk in-off rand lea weigh hub out thus sin thought, tanned peg lets head, “Defuse he water mien, pew,” wand pews head, “Hits Jess twat eye thin come eyes elf, peg lit,” tanned peg lets head, “Button thee yaw there rand, pew, him host rim amber,” rand pews head, “Kwai troop peg lit haul though eye head fur gotten nit four thumb owe mint.”

Tanned thin, jesters thick aim toothy sick spine trice, pew lucked rowan two seethe hat know buddy hell swizzle lessening, hints head dinner fairies hull am vice: “Peg lit tie huffed aside deeds hum thin.”

“Water viewed aside deed, pew?”

“Eye hove aside head took hatch awe heifer lump.”

Pew know daddy said sever all thymes assays head thus, sand weigh Ted four peg lit whose hay “howe?” ore “Pew yoke who dint!” terse hum thin gulp fill off thought cert, butt peg lots head know thin.

Thief act worse peg lit wore swishing thought head thaw tab out tit fir.

"Sty shell dough hit," Sid Pugh, waft her weigh tingle idyll hunger, "buy mean suffered wrap. Panned atom most beer canning traps hoe Yule laughter hell up mi, peg lit."

"Pews," head peg lit, filling quiet tap pier gain how, "Eye wall."

Land thin hiss head, "House shell widow wit?" end pews head, "thoughts jest hit. Howe?"

Wand thin this hat dawn tug heather two thin kit tout.

Pews furs tide ear whiz thought this shed digger ferried heap it, tend thin though heifer lump wood comb awl long end foal inn though pet, tanned—

"Wise?" head peg lit.

"Wye watts?" head pew.

"Wye woody foal lin?

Pure hub bed hiss knows withers pa winds head thought thee heifer lump mite bee wok king all hung, gumming awl idylls hung, end lieu king a pot thus Kay wand her ring effete wood drain, ends sew we wooden seethe ferried heap hit hunt Tillie whiz have weighed own, win net wood bite who'll hate.

Peg loots head thought the Swiss hay fairy goad wrap, butts opposing eat wear reign nun awl red dye? Poor hub diss knows sag hen, nuns head thought tea head dent thaw tough thought.

End thin Hebe right end hop, pinned Sid thought, effete wear reigning awl red dye, thee heifer lump wood bill-hook king hat this Kay wandering effete wood Clare rope panned sew hew wood dents heath he ferried heap hit ton Tillie whiz huff weighed own … wen knit wood bee tool hate.

Peg lots head thought, know thought thus paw went hid bean axe planed, death ought tit whiz sick honing trop.

Thus car little litter, No than yell law though run

Thud whore off though jay ill bean flan go pin frame with inn their up eared, din though fur rest plaice, lie cab lack shed hoe am margin inn two this Hun's shy in, though groom mend grizzly presents off that own be dull, withers horde buyers hide, end hiss Taff off off a sinner sand.

Thus purse on age proof fig your dinned wrap present head inners ass pecked thee holed his mulls a very tea off though pure it tannic ode off lore, witch hit whiz hiss busy nest who add Minnie stir inn nits finer land claw set tap location toothy off end her.

Strut chain fourth Theo fish hulls Taff inn hiss lift tanned, heel aid hiss rite a pone thus shawl door rough hay hung woo man, who math huss drow fur word, ant hill, lone though thrush old off though prise on dour, sheer rappelled hymn, bine act shin marque twee thin hat churl dig gnat eye end fours off car actor, rand steppe tint who though owe pin hair has off buyer rowan free-wheel.

Shea bow runner harms itch aisled, dab bay be off sum thrum anthers sold, hue inked tanned tern diss hide hits let all phase frame that who've avid lie toughed hay; big horse sits axe his tense, hear two four, rid brow tit tack wain tense sewn lea withy grate while late Ovid dun Joan, know wrath third arcs home up art mint off though pry son.

Whin they hung woo man—thumb other off thus chilled—stud fool ear a field beef whore thick rowed, debts seamed two beer furs Tim pulse tickle hasp thee in font close lea two wear boo sum; knots hoe match buy Ann imp else off math early off action, nest hat shim mite their bike Huns heeler sir tent hoe kin, witch whiz raw turf ass end din toured wrasse.

Inner mow mint tow ever why sledge Hadj gin thought wan offer shim wood butt purely surf too wide dun other, sheet hook though bay bee honor harm, mend wither burr nimble hush, shinned yeti whore teas mile, land dug lance thought wooden aught bee yob bashed, luck dare hound attar tow wins peep hole land neigh burrs. Sun though brass tough for Gowan, nun fain read claw with, Sir Roundhead with anal a bore writ hem brow Derry hand fanned a stick flower ashes off goaled three head, up eared they'll let her 'hay'.

Hit whiz sew art his tickle hay dun, end wits home hutch fur Tillie tie hand gore Jess luck sure eye ants off antsy, thought tit addle thee off hacked offal lass dinned fit tongued echo ration toothy up peril witch he whore, rand witch whiz offers splay indoor inn hack hoard ants withy Tay stove though wage, butt grate lea bee yawned watt whiz all loud buy thus hump jury rig you'll hay shins off thick colon knee. They hung woo man whist hall, withy fig you rough purr fact tell a gant son ale urges kale. Shed arc hand hob bun dent air, sew glassy thought tit through of this hunch chine wither glee; Amanda fey switch, bees hides bean be you tough full frame rig you'll are it tea off eat sure sand wretch ness off camp lack shin, head thee hymn press sieve ness off bill longing two hum arced brew end dip lack ice.

Shoe whistle aid eel hike, two, waft her thumb manor rough thee famine nine gin Tillie tee-off though stays; car wreck tore iced buyers hurt hens Tate hand dig gnat hear other thin buy thud hell lack hate, Evan ness ant, tanned dinned risk rye babble grays witches know wreck Hogan iced assets sinned dick hay shin. Hand Nev veer rid hiss tarp run up eared moor laid deal hike, inn thee aunt teak inter prat hay shin off that harm, then ash he is sued frame though prise on. Though sue had biff whore no nor, rand hid axe peck Ted tub a holed herd him dinned hobs cured buyer diss aster risk loud, wear ass tone gnashed, tend eve an star tilled, two purr sieve vow herb you tea show now't, handmaid ah hail owe off though miss far tune end dig know Minnie inn witch he whiz sinful loped.

Atom hay beet truth hat, tours hens at tough hob server, their whiz hum thin axe quiz Italy pay in full inn net. Hair rat ire, witch end heed, shed rat four thee hock Asian inn prise on, end dad muddled mutt chaff tore heroine fans see, seamed two whacks press thee hat he chewed offers parrot, thud despair rate wreck lesson ness offer mooed, buy hits while dinned pick chew risk pick Yule ear ratty. Butt though poynt twitched rue awl ice, sand, asset wear, trains fig gourd thaw airer—sew thought bow thumb hen end whim manhood bean fame ill eye are leak wain Ted we thus tarp prune wear know hump rest ass off the hay bee hell door four though firs thyme—whiz thoughts cal little hatters owe Fanta stick alley amber Roy dirt tinned a lumen ate head a pone herb ooze hum. Met hid thee off act offer spelt aching hair rout off Theo ore dinner hay rill lay shins wit you Manny tea, end ink losing heron ass fear buy hearse elf.

Thee hay Jove inner cents, seed death wore ton

Missed her bow farts he crate, peephole wear rug greed, whiz though weigh hick harried thin. Soffit worse awl fairy welt who wisp hair thought tea hid bean 'hell pit' tool heave ingle hand buy thin turn ash shown all ban king how's sin witch head bean numb ploy Yid; hick harried doff thought rue moor ass sees alley ass there wrest—thon ewe Yorick's busy ness cons high ants wiz Noel Hess hens it hive thin nits morels tanned hard—hick harried aver eye thin biff whore hymn, handle gnu Yorick kin two hiss ed raw wing rheum, sand four rover twin tea ears know peephole heads head thee wear 'go wing toothy bow farts' withies aim tow naff sick you ratty ass sieve the heads head the wore go wing tomb missed man's son Ming hot, sand withy had dads hatters faction naff no wing the wood gat tot can vast beck dux invent age whines, sins Ted oft hep head view Vic lick owe with hout aye ear rand wormed hop croak hits frame fill a Delphi are.

Misses bow fart, thin, head issue Sewell up eared dinner bucks joust biff whore though Jew walls Hong; hand whin, no gain ass you Sewell, sheer hose sat thee yen dove thee thawed hacked, rue are hopper rack low cab outer love lease shoal doors, sand is up peered, gnu Yorick new thought mint thought huff on our lay tore though bawl wood big in.

Thee bow farts souse whiz wan thought gnu Yorick hers swear prowed toes hoe two fore runners, asp pish alley yawn thin height off thee anew wall bowl. Though bow farts sad bin hum hong thee furze tip peephole lin gnu Yorick two hone there hone read fell fit car pet tanned hove a troll lid dawn this taps buy there rowan fit main, Hun door there rowan earning, gains Ted off firing hit withies upper rand thee bawl rheum cheers.

Thee add dulse Owen augur hated thick host tum offal lit tin they'll aid dust hake there cull oaks of inn thee all, lin stead off show filling apt who thee hoes Tessa's sped rheum end rick hurling there air withy hay duff though gasp earner; bow fart wizen doors two do hoves head thought hiss opposed dollies why fuss frenzied made sues aught two wit thought the wear prop early quaff feed whin they'll eft tome.

Thin thee how sad bean bowled leap land withy bawl rheum, sew thought, tins Ted doves quizzing threw an arrow pass sage tug het twit (asset thatch ever says) wan mar chits so limb lea dough knave is tar off fen full aided raw wing rums (this he grin, thick rims son anther boot on door), sea yin frame off are thumb manic handled lust whores rough lack Ted din thee poll lashed park cattery, yawned bee yawned thought thud debt thus suffer cone serve a Tory work ham meal ears sand reef earns are chit there coast leaf owe liege owe verse heats off blackened goaled bum boo.

Gnu lined art shore, ass beck home merry hung manor vis pose sessions, trolled din sum wattle ate. Head lefties hover cote withies ilk's tock Inga'd few tum hen (this talk kings wear wan off bow farts phew fat you wit tease), sad odd ill dough isle inn though lie brewer airy young wits pan ash slither rand four gnashed wit bowl land mall ache height, weary phew main watch hat ting ant put anon there Dan sing loves, sanded fine alley joy end though lie-in off guess 'tis who misses bow fart whiz race heaving awn though thresh holed off thick rim sun drow win rheum.

Arch her whiz diss tinkle in her vas. Head knot Gowan beck two hiss claw boff tour Theo pair (ass thee hung blurred sue Sewell eyed hid), butt, thin height bean fain, hid wall kid furs hummed hiss stance sup 5th have anew biff whore tern nun beckon thud erection off though bow fart souse. Hie wiz deaf finite lie off raid thought thumb Ming hot smite big hoeing two fair; thought, tin faked, thumb height hove grainy Ming hot sword hers tube wring thick Cohen Tessa Len's cart who though bawl.

Frame thought own off thick lob ox head purse heaved dhow gray vim ass take thought wood beyond, tho' hie wiz moor thin never deter manned two's "heath a thin threw", heave felt loss shiver lass lea he gore touch sham peon hiss bee troth thuds cozen thin beef whore there Brie if torque cat Theo parry.

Toss off thud herb burr villas, Tum ass Sard Dee

Though villa Jove ma lot lame hid though no wrath ease stern nun Jew lay shins off though Bude awful veil off bleak moor orb lack more a fours head, end in girdled ants sick clue dead ridge eon, forth ham host par ton trod dinners shat bite our wrist tore lance cape ain't her, thaw a thinner fore ours jar knee frame land in. Nit tizzy fail lose sack wain tents hiss pest maid bye few Wingate frame this hum mitts off though wills, thoughts around debt—tax apt purr raps Jew ring thud routs huffs hummer.

Anon guy dead ram bull in two wits rice hisses sin bawd whether receipt twin gender diss hatters faction withy hits gnaw row, taught you us, sand Marie whey's.

Thus fur tile land shell toured racked off can tree, inn witch though feels Aaron ever brawn end this prink sin averred rice boned did awn this sow with buy though bowled chaw courage thought hum braces though prow men Nancy' off ham bull din ill, bulb harrow, net tall camped out, dug berry, eyes toy, yawned bobbed town.

Thought reveler frame thick host, stew, waft her plow din nor eth word four risk whore off my ills owe veer cull serious down sand carnal hands, had hen layer each his they've urge off wan off thee suss carp mints, his sir prized handle light head tuber holed, axe tended lie come hap bean Neath hymn, Mick Hun treed if faring abs hole Ute lea frame thought twitchy asp assed threw.

Bee hind dim thee ills soar rope in, this Hun play sized own up on feel lids sew largesse tug hive anon closed car actor toothy lance cape, they'll lay inns sore why it, though edges slow wimple ash head, thee at most sphere cull earl less.

Herein they've alley, thaw hurled seams tubby cans tract head up honors mall errand moored deli Kate's kale; they've heeled sore me ear pad ducks, whore add juiced thought frame thus site there edge rouse sup peer run knit work oft hark grin though reds owe verse up ridding though pay leer grin off thug wrasse.

Thee atom mows fear bin heath this slang whore us, Sandy's hoe tin Jude withers your thought watt tart tests cull thumb idyll diss stance part aches soul sew off that Hugh, wile thee whore eyes on bee yawned hiss off thud heap pest stool tram marine.

Are Hubble hand sore phew handle him mitt head; wit butts light axe hep shins though prose pecked tizzy browed wretch mess hove gross entries, man tooling mine whore ills sinned hails with inn thumb age horse. Hutches they've ail off hob lack more.

A say yawn nay chewer, Alf walled hoe emir sun

Their hard haze switch shock heron thus climb hate, tat awl must anise he's on-off thee ear, wear inn though whirled riches sits purr faction, wen thee hair, thee Evan lea buddies, sand thee err thumb ache awe harm money, ass sieve nay chewer wooden dull jar roughs prang, wen, inn this bull leak up ass hides off though plan net, no thinners two dick lair thought weave herd off though happy yeast latter chewed, sand wee Basque kin though shy nun ours off Laura deigned queue bar, wen aver eye thin thought hassle lie if gyves high naff sat hiss faction, end thick hat till thought lion thug round seam two wave grate hand train quell thaw wits.

This hall see yawns maybe lucked four wither lit all morass your ants sin thought pew wear rock tow bare whether, witch weed ass tongue wish buy thin aim off finned Ian's hummer.

Thud hay, him mesh your ably lungs, leaps owe veer though braw wed ills sand worm feel lids. Two hovel lift threw wall lights honey yours, seams lunge ever tea in huff.

This holy Terry plaices dune knot seam quiet lone lea. Hat thug hates off though four rest, this her priced manner though whirled does four stool heave hiss hit tea yes tum mates off grate hands mall, why sand full lash. Thin naps hack cuff cussed hum foals offers beck wit though firs tap hymn aches sinter thee spree sinks. Hear ass hank tit eye witch aims sour reel edge Huns, sand reel lit hay witch desk red hits sour hear roes.

Hear wife hind nay chewer tubby though circus stand cess switched wharves sever rye others her comes stance, hinge had jostle hiker gad awl month hat comb two hair. Weave crypt tout hover claws sink row did douses sin two thin height tinned moaning, end wee sea watt mow jest hick beaut tease dale leer rap puss inn there booze hum.

Howell ling Louis wood ass cape though bar rears switch rend earth thumb camp Harry Tivoli imp Poe tent, ass cape this off fist tick hay shin hands sack honed though tins huffer neigh chewer two hunt rants suss. That hemp herd lie tough thaw hoods hiss lie carp perp pet you all moaning, end hiss Tim you'll hating gander owe wick. Thee hain chant leery port heads pales off though plaice scree pup awn huss.

This steams off pie inns, Himmel lox, sand dough cuss, sol must glee mill Ike eye Ron awn thee axe height Ted eye. Though ink commune a cable trice bed inn two purr suede dust who leave wit thumb, mend quitter lie five sole limb try files.

Hear know whist Tory, yore chewer chaws stay 'tis hint her poll lay Ted don thud dive hi in ski end thee hymn more tally ear.

Hah we silly whim might wok awn word din two whoa pinning lance cape, abs orbed bine you pick chewers, sand buy thaw its fests acceding ghee chaw there, runt hill bide agrees their wreck hull action off foam whisk rowed a doubt off thumb hind, doll mammary hub literate head buy that heron knee off though press ant, hand wee whirl head dint rye oomph bine nay chewer. Thee sin chant mincer mad is anal, this owe burr rand eel louse.

The sour plane please yours, kine Leanne hay tiff two wuss. Wick home tour rowan, end may cough rends wit mat hair, witch they ambit yes chat tore off this cools wood purr suede ass two diss pies. Wean ever comport withy; thumb hind luff sits sold ohm; mass what her tour Thor wrist, sew whiz there hock, thug round, tour ice, sand ands, sand fit. Titters farm what her: writ hiss scold flay him: watt well thaw, hot a fin nutty!

Aver a no willed fray end, defer lie cud ear fray end inn broth her, wen witch hat effect addle he wits strain jaws, scum sin these owe nest phase, sand hakes sag rave lubber tea wee thus, sand Seamus suss sow tough fern nun since. Hit is given hot thee hew manse hen cess rue men huff.

Wig hoe aught day lea end knight lea tough heed thee ice sun thee whore eyes on, end rack choirs home hutches cope, jesters wean knead what her four orb hath. Their a role dig grease off gnat Ural lin flue wince, frame thee square ant tin paw worse off neigh chew, erupt tour dearie stand gray vest Minnie stray shins toothy him Madge inn nation end though sole.

Their hiss though buck hat off coaled what her frame this purr ring, though hood fie writ who witch thatch hilled ravel leer ushers force save tea—yawned their hiss this hob lime aural off aught hum end off new in.

Win ness sill lin neigh chewer, rand roar live vine asp arrow cites frame hair hoots sing rains, sand weir ass sieve gland says frame though Evan lea bawdy, switch callous two Saul itch hood, dinned fort hell their emote test few chewer. Though blew Zen eth hiss though poi in tin witch row manse sand rhea lit team heat.

Threw many nib oat, Jar Rome cage a roam

Their wharf whore off fuss—Jaw edge, in Twill yams Ham mule Harries, sand mice elf, fanned Manned more rent sea. Wee worse hitting inn mire rheum, sum mow king, ant hawking hob bout tow bade wee wear—bade frame am head deckle poi ant off hue eye me naff coarse. Wee war roll fee lung sea day, end wee wear get tang whiten err Vassar bow tit.

Tarry's head duff felled Satch heck straw horde din airy Fitz off gid din ness scum mow veer rim mat thymes, thought tea hair dull lean new watt hew ass dew wing; gunned thin jaw wedges head thought tea head Fitz off gid din nest two, wand whored lean new watt TEA whist who wing. Wit meat whiz mile lover thought whiz outer void dare.

Eye new wit whiz mile lover thought whiz outer void dare, bee course sigh hid joust bean rhea din gap aye tent lover pulls sir queue lore, inn witch weird debt hailed they've airy us sum tomes buy witch hum ankh hoot hell wen hiss lover whiz sow tough awed her. Eye head thumb maul.

Hit hiss hum host tacks tray horde inner eye thin, bat eye nave are head up hate tent mad ice sun add veer 'tis mint wit hout bean prop hell lid tooth thicken clue shin thought eye yams offering frame though part tick you lard a seize their inn dell tow within nits must fir you leant farm. Thud high hag nose is seam sin ever reek haste hook horror Spandex act lea wit haul this hen say shins thought eye hove aver fell. Tire rim amber go wing toothy brit ask mew seem wand hay tour rid hop that tree tum mint fours hums light tail mint off witch eye adit hutch—chafe ever, rife an say a t'was.

Eye gut Dow win though buke, canned dread awl Ike aim tour heed; an thin, inn Ann nun thin kin mow mint, eye eye dilly tern head though lives, sand big hand two win dole leant lea stud did as eases, gin orally. Eye four got twitch whiz though firs test hamper ripe lunged dint who—sum fir Phil, diva stating scow urge, aye no—wand, bee four eye head gland said huffed own though Liszt tough "prim money Tories hymn tums," sit whiz born inn up pawn math hat eye hid fare league hot hit. Ice hat furry wile, fro sun wit whore roar; rand thin, inn though lest lass ness oft hasp pair, eye hug gain tern Dover though pay jazz. Ike aim toot hive void fee veer—red this hymn toms—desk covered thought eye head hive void fee veer, muss tough head hit four man thus with hout no wing hit—wand herd watt tell sighed gat; tern dupes ain't vie toast hence.

Eye fawned, dizzy hacks peck Ted, thought eye head thought who, beg ant hug het inter rested din mike ace, sand eat her mined two sieve tit toothy but tome, mince hoes tart Ted Alf abet tickle lea—red upper goo, handle earned thought eye whiz hick anon ferret, hand thought thee hack cute stay jaw wood come mince sinner bout an nether fort knight. Bore eights Dee cease, eye whiz rill leaved two fined, eye hid own lea inner mud divide farm, hands owe fair ass thought whiz cones earned, dime mite leave furry ears. Collar a high head, wits a veer come pluck hay shins; sand hip there eye a ice seamed two hove bean borne wit. Thigh plow did conch she yen shoes lea, threw that when tease hicks let hers, sand thee own lea ma lady Ike hood conk lewd eye head knot gat whiz souse may Disney.

Sieve ill diss owe bead yens, Hen read have hid Though row, 1849

Eye hove pay dunno pole tacks four sex yours. Eye wasp hut tint who wedge ale wants sun thus sick count, four wan height; tanned, ass ice stewed cons hid a ring thaw alls off sullied stow win, too worth reef heat the hick, thud whore off would end eye run, off hoot the hick, end thee eye run great teen witches trained they'll height, Ike hood knot tell up beans truck withy full lash ness off thought tins tat you chin witch tree Ted mere see fie worm ear flash shinned blowed end bow inns, tubby looked top.

Eye wandered thought hitch hood huff can clue did hat Len thought thud whiz though Bess chews sit cooed putt meat who, wand head Nev ear thaw two have ale lets elf off mice surf ices sins hum weigh. Ice haw thought, tiff their whiz awe all luffs tone bet wean mean dumb eye tow wins men, their whiz ass till moored if heck cult want hook lime moor brake threw biff whore thick hood gat tubby ass freeze eye worse.

Sighed hid knot furry mow mint fill can find, dinned thaw alls seamed hug rate waist off stow nun more tar. High fault 'tis a fie all loan offal mote hounds men hid pay dumb eye tacks. The hay plane lead hid knot know-how two tree tummy, bat bee have dull Ike purse sins whore run door bread. Din a very thread tanned a very camp lea mint there whiz able under; forth hay thawed thought Mitch he if diss hire whist whose tanned Theo there sighed off though grates tone whole. Ike hood knot bats mile two's he howe wind us tree us Leith hale hocked thud whore awn mime head at hay shuns, switch fall owed thumb outer gain with hout letter hind rants, sand the wear reel lea haul thought whist deign jar us.

Ass thick hood knot wretch chummy, the head wrasse solved two pun ash may buddy; joust ass buoys, off thick can knot comets hump parson hug hence tomb the hove ass pie twill lab use hissed hog. Ice haw thought this Tate whiz have-wet head, thought tit whist hymn Midas all own womb man withers hill verse puns, sand thought hit deed knot no wits France fro mitts foe, sand aisle loss tall mire hum mane angry specked four hit, end pit heed hit.

The ass thus Tate Nev ear runt tent shill leak Hun France sum manse hence sin till heck chew alley arm aural, bat tone lea hiss buddy, hiss census. Sit hiss knot harmed wits you peer Eeyore witter on nasty, bat wits who peer ear fuss sickles string eth. Eye whiz knot borne tubby four.

Sty well Brie though oft her may yawn fash shun. Lettuce he Hughie's this straw in gust. Watt fours Hess sum altitude? The yawn leak kin fours Smee Hugh owe bear rye hurl loath thin eye. The fours meat who big home lick thumbs elves.

Eyed who knot ear off man bean fours tool hive thus sway ore thought buy misses off mean. Watts aught offal hive wear thought tool heave?

Whin eye meat hag go varmint twitches hays tomb he, 'yaw moan knee oar yawl hive,' wish hood eye bean hays tug Yvette mime honey? Yet maybe inner grates tray tanned knot no watt hood who: Ike kin knot hell up thought.

Atom host tell pits elf; dew whiz eyed who. Hit hiss knot wear though wile twos navel lab bout tit.

High yam knot rasp puns sable forth he suck cess fool war king off thumb ash sheen nary off sew sigh at tea. High yam knot thus sun off thee hen gin ear. Eye purse heave thought, whin a neigh corn end itch hest nut foals hide buys hide, thee wand hose knot rum mane Ann nerd tomb ache weigh forth he oath there, bat bow though bay there rowan loss, hand-spring end grue wand flour ashes baste thick an, tell wan, perch ands, sew verse shad owes sand wrist Roy's Theo there. Off hip planet can knot leave hack cord dint tune hay chewer, writ dice; sands hoe hum an.

Theo'd vent yours off Hack all brief fin, Mar rucked wain, 1884

You'd owned no hub hout mew with hout chew hover red hub buke buy thin aim off Theo'd vent yours oft hums saw your; bat thought hain to know mutter. Thought buke whiz maid buy mist harm arced wain, end hit old that Ruth mane lea.

Their whist thin switch hiss straight shed, bat mane lea hit tolled that Ruth. Thought hiss no thin. Guy Nev ears e'en any buddy battle eyed want thyne more in other, with hout tit whiz ant Paul Lear thaw hid dough, worm hay beam airy. Ant pall lea—Tum's ant poll leash he hiss—sand merry, end thaw hid dough dug lasses salt holed hub bout tin thought buke, witch hiss mows tall lea hat rue buke, wits hum stray chores, ass eyes head biff whore.

Know thee weigh thought though buke wines sup piss thus: tum end miff hound thumb honey thought there hob burrs sedan though Kay fanned debt maid huss wretch. Wig hot sex thou sand hollers sup peace—soul goaled. Debt wizen awe fools height off moan knee wen knit worse pie led dap. Will, Judd jaw thatch her hit hook kitten putt tit tout hat tint wrest, tanned hit fat shed huss sad holler add hay op peace sole they ear hound—moor thinner buddy cud till watt two'd who eth. Thaw hid dough hug lass sheet hook miff whore hearse Hun, end dull eyed show woods civil eye Smee; bat tit whiz ruff leaving inn thee how sole that thyme, cans hid her ring howe diss mall rig you'll lair rand he scent thaw hid dough whiz sin awl hair whey; sands hoe whin Ike hood dents tanned debt knoll hunger, aisle hit tout.

Eye gat tint whom eye holed drags sand mice you gore hugs heed hug gain, end whiz fray ends hatters fight. Bat tum saw Yuri Hun Ted mea yap pans head dew whiz go wing two's tart tub and offer hob burrs, sand aim height jaw win off eye wood gob hack tooth thaw hid dough wend beer ass peck table. Sew eye when tub hack.

Thaw hid dough shook rye Dover mean culled mere pearl last lam, mend chic hauled meal hot off father neigh mist who bat shine ever mint know warm buy yet. Ship putt mean thumb nuke loathes sag hen, end eye coo dent dune know thin bats wet ends wet, tinned fee loll cram pit hop.

Wealth hen, Theo willed thin come hence dug hen. Thaw hid dough run gab hell force up her, end chew wad took home two thyme. Whin ewe gut two that able ewe could dent gore height tweet, batch chew head two white four thaw hid dough toot tacked owner red end groom bull all lit tell lover thaw vitals, thaw there warn not relay hen knee thin thumb hatter wit thumb—thought hiss, know thin known lea a very thin worse coo kit buy hits elf. Inner bar roll laugh add sun hence sitters duff are rent; thins gat Mick's stop, pinned thaw Jews kine duffs wops a round, end though thins gob better.

Aft hearse up her shoe gut tout herb hook end learn dumb he hob bout Mow says sand thee Bull rashers, sand eye whiz sinners wet two fined hout taller bout Tim; bat buy hand buy shill ate tit tout thought Mow says sad binned head dick hence hid a rabble thyme; sew thin eyed hid dent car know moor rob hout hymn, big horse sigh doughnut ache noose tock kind head peephole.

Pretties sue when eye won't head toss moke, kind dusk kit thaw hid dough tool het tummy. Bat shoe wood dent. Shoes heady t'was hum me imp racked hiss, sand wore sent cull lean, end eye massed wry tune knot dew wit tinny moor.

Thought hiss jest though hay wits hump peephole. The gat dow nun nothing when thud owned no know thin hub out tit. Hear shoe whiz hub other ring hub hout mow says, switch whiz know keen tour, rand know youse two any buddy, bean go news sea, het fine ding up owe are off holt wit may ford dew winger thin thought heads hum goo din knit.

Tend sheet hooks naff two; off cores thought whiz sole rite, big horse shed doughnut hearse elf. Hearse hiss tore, mess Swats hone, at holler rubble Slee mould made, wit gaggles son, head joust comet who'll hive wither, runt hook asset tit mean how withers spell lung buke. Shoe wore kid maim idyll ling erred four a bout tin our, rand thin thaw hid dough may door he's sup. Ike hood dense stewed hit match languor.

Thin furry no were hit worse dead lead hull, land eye whiz feed jet tea. Mess Swats hone woods hay, 'Dough want putsch shore fee top their, Hackle bury' end 'Dough wants crunch chap lick thought, Hackle buries hit tops trait' tend prat tissue win shoe woods hay 'Dough want gape penned straight itch lick thought Hackle bury—wide dent shoot rite who bee hive?'

Thin sheet hold may yawn hub bout thee bard plaice, sand eyes head eye washed eye whiz their. Shoe gat mud thin, bat eyed hidden tomb e'en know warm.

Haul eye won Ted whiz tug hoe sum wares; haul eye wont hid whiz hat chain jaw eye war ant pert hick you'll are.

Shoes head at whiz wick head twos hay watt ice heads; head shoe wood ants hay yet four though hole whirled; shoe whiz go wing tool hive sew west who goat who thug hood plaice.

Wally coo dent sea know wad vent age gin go wing ware shoe whiz go wing, sew eye maid dap mime hind eye wood dent rife fur hit. Batten eye Nev ears head sew, big horse sit wood dough win lea may kit rub bull, land wood dent dune nag hood.

Tars Ann, Headgear ice borrows

Eye head thus Tory frame wan Hugh wad know busy ness toot hell lit tomb he, ore two hinny owe there. Eye make red it this add ducked tough inn flue whence off inn knolled vent age up on thinner rater four though big inning off fit, tanned may yawns kept tickle inn crud you lit tea Jew ring thud hays thought fall lowed four thee ball lance off this tray hinge tail.

Whin make Hun viva yell hosed ass covered thought head tolled mice home hutch, end thought eye wasp rowan two dow tough full ness, hiss fuel lush pried ass you mid that ask Theo willed vent age hid come minced, tanned sew we Hun hearth tree tin never dents inn though for muff must hay man you script, tanned rye a fish hill wreck hordes off though Brit ash coal loan eel off face two sup port Manny off this ale lea hint feet yours off hiss rum ark Hubble nor rat tough.

Eyed dew knots hay this Tory hiss strew, four eyed hid knot twit ness though happy nuns witch hit port raise, bat though fecht thought tin thought hell lung off fit two ewe eye hove tack in feck tissue sun aims four though prints supple car actors quiet's office shun Tillie off may hoe win bee leaf thought tit may beet rue.

They hello, mill dewed pay jazz off thud dire he off Oman longed head, end their accords off thick hollow kneel off iced huff tale purr feck Tillie withy narrate hive off make con viva yell hosed, inns hoe guff ewe this Tory ass eye panes take king lea pees tit tout frame thee sever roll very us sage ant sees. A few dew knot fined attic red able ewe wheel lot list bee ass wan wit may inn knack no ledge gin thought titties you nick, rum ark able, land inter resting.

Frame their heck cords off thick colon eel off ice sand frame thud head manse die airy will earn thought aye hung ingle ash know bull man, loom wish shell cull jaw ink laden, law word grace toke, whisk hum miss shunned tomb ache up pack Yule your lea deli cut inn vest tug hay shun off conned dish Huns inner brit ash whist coos tough free can colon knee frame who sample neigh tough fin habit ants sin other you rope he Ann paw wear whiz none tube beer rack rooting soul Jew wears four writs neigh tough farm me, witch a choose id soul leaf or though four sable cull action offer hub burr rand die very frame this have edge try bus sole hung thick hung go wend thee are you whim me.

Thin neigh toughs off though brit ash cull Annie camp lined thought men knee off there yang many wear rent iced to weigh threw thumb middy yam off hair angle owing prom ices, Bat thought phew a fanny aver rat earned two there foam holies.

Thee ingle ash Menin off rick awe when tea van fur theirs, hay hing thought this spoor bull lacks swear hell din virtue walls sleigh very, sins softer there tear rums a final list mint hex pyre dither rig nor rants whiz imp hosed up pun buy there why toff fussers, Anther wart hold thought the add jets ever all yours twos surf.

End sew thick hollow kneel off ice sup pointed jaw wink laid on tour knew posed tin whist off rick are, bat hiss cone fed dent chill lin struck shuns scent turd honor though row win vest tag hay shun off thee Hun fare treed mint off bull lack brit ashes objects buy Theo fuss sirs off offer end lea you rope peen paw wore. Wye hew whiz scent hiss sow ever offal idyll mow mint two thus Tory, four e'en ever maiden nun vest tug hay shun, or, inn fecht, daddy aver each hiss dust tin nation.

Clay tone whiz that hype off ingle ash man thought wan licks Bess two ass sew see hate withy know bull list man you mints off hiss tore rick itch heave mint up honor thou sinned Vic Tory yes bottle fields—ass strung veer rile men, mint tally, more alley, end physique alley.

Inns tat sure hew ass sob hove thee aver rage high, 'tis sighs swag ray, hiss fee chewers rig you'll are ends strung, hiss car rage thought off purr fecht, robe bus stealth thin flew winced buy hiss yours a farm meat raining.

Paw lit tickle lamb bush shun head coursed hymn two sick trains fur rants frame thee harm me tooth he colon eel off fuss sand sew he fined hymns, Tillie hung, enter rusted wither deli cut tanned imp whore tent come mission nun this air vice off thick wean.

Whinny race heaved thus sup point mint hew ass bow the late head dinned up hauled. Though proof air mints seamed two hymn inn thin hay chewer off owe hell-merry Ted dree word four panes taking end dint hell agent surf face, sand assist Epping's tone tip hosts off grate rim port hence sand respond Sybil a tea, baton Theo their Andy head bin mar reed two thee on gnaw rabble alleys rather furred fours care sillier 3 man thus, sand debt whiz though though toughed hay king thus fairy hung gurl lint who thud hain Jew whirrs sand eye sew lay shun oft rap pick hell laugh rick car thought up hauled dim.

Four hairs ache key wood haver a fused Theo point mint, batch he wood knot avid sew. Winced head shin suss Ted thought tea hack sipped, dinned, dinned heed, ticker wee thumb.

Their worm others sand broth hers sands his terse sand cuss sins two axe press very ass sup pinions sun this object, bat ass two watt these ever alley had vise dust Tory ass high lent.

Winnow own lea the tone hub right Maim awning innate teen ate tea ate, jaw win, lured graze toke, canned laid he alleys hailed framed over run there weigh two off rick haw.

Hum on the lay tore the are hived hat fur rhea tow in wear the itch art heard ass mauls hailing vassal, thee few welder, witch whiz tube air thumb tooth hair fine knelled hest tin nation.

End a fence off womb man, Itch hell Mink kin

Mean, ass aver rhea wan nose, soared ass posed two quest shun thus appear rear inn tell agents off womb men; there he goat is him dumb hands thud Dean aisle, land theirs hell dumb riff fleck toughen off two diss pose off fit bile lodge hick cull land evade dent shell anal lasses.

Mow rover, wrasse wish Elsie hub it lay tore Ron, there Izzy's pea shoe sup peer rants off sow wind ness sin there paws ash shun; the hove four stop pun womb men inn art off fish shill car actor witch whelk on seals there eel car actor, rend womb men huff hound debt prow fit table twin carriage thud ass sip shin.

Bat tho' a very gnaw mall men this chair ashes this who thin hunk shun thought tea hiss thee inn tell lacked you all sue peer ear rough fall womb men, end part tick you'll early offers why if, hick Huns Stan Tillie gaffs though lye two wisp retention bike on soul tin end off airing two watt hick halls hair inn chew wish shun.

Thought test whose hay, Hun nose buy axe pee rhea hints thought hair judge mint tin men knee mutters off cap at all cans Ernie's moors hut till lands urchin thin hiss sewn, hand, bee end hiss sink lined two hack red it thus grate her saga city two hum whore camp pet ant tin tell agents, seat aches riff huge bee hind thud hocked run thought titties Jew twosome imp penny trouble land dint tan Jew bull tall ant four gassing core act lease humph Hague (an dun ness since, in fro' you man) nuns tin kit.

That ruin neigh chewer off thus all edged dins tin kit, ho waver, hiss ray veal lid bine axe parry mint off thus hit you way shuns switch chins pyre Oman took haul lit two hiss hayed. This hit shoe way shuns dune hotter eyes owe tough thee poorly tack nickel probe blooms thought tore hissed hay leak Huns earn, bat tout off there airer rand moor fonder mental, land dense sin or muscle lea moored iffy cult probe blooms switch bee set hymn own lea hat lung end are egg you lore in tore vales, sing hoe off fur rat hest, knot off hiss smear cap acidy four be ender hilled, bat off hiss cap acidy four gin you wine ratio sin nation.

Gnomon, night hake hits, hay I've wan can schuss lea yin fear Eeyore rand den Pict, wood can salt hiss why foe bout tiring hick lark, core rub out axe tend ink red hit twosome pall trek cuss tomb her, roar rub out summer rue teen peace huffed Audrey's wind ling; baton hot tea van thumb host Teague go whist tick min wood fey ill twos hound this sent tum meant offers why if hub out aching up art near in two hasp busy ness, sore a bouts tan ding four pub lick off ice, sore hub out comb batting Hun fare rand rue win huss camp petition, ore rub or mar rye yin guff third ought tore. Satch thin guess sore off mass heave imp aught ants;

they'll eye hat though found hay shun off Welby yin; thick hall four though baste that thought thumb an can frond Ted buy thumb kin master; though payrolls Sid din inner rung diss seize shun owe veer comb he van thick clam mores off van knit tea.

Hit hiss sins hutch sit you weigh shuns thought this appear rear men till lug rasp off womb men hiss a fob vie yes shoot hilly tea, end huss two bead mitt head.

Hit hiss ear thought there eyes sob hove thins heck knee fuss scent scent a men tally teas, hoop purse Titian's sand for mew lea off min, end apple eye toothy busy ness there sing Yule art all lint fours hep a rating Theo peer ants frame this hubs stance, sands hoe whack sirs eyes watt hiss culled there rent you wish shun.

In tuition? Withal rasp pecked, bash! Thin knit worse sin tuition thought lead are win two wore cow it thee high Poe this is off gnat sure all sell action. Thin knit worse sin tuition thought fabric hated thee joy ant tickle lea camp licks core off 'Devil Curie.' Thin knit worse sib tuition thought convenes hid call hum bus off thee axe hiss tents offal hand whist off their sores.

Haul off the sin tuition off witch sew match trance sinned dent tall rub ashes mare chanted a snow moor rand knoll Hess thin nun tell agents—hint hell agents soak e'en thought tit kin penny trait toothy hid dent Ruth threw thumb host four mid double rapping's off falls hem bill ants sand deem mean our, rand soul idyll car wrapped head buy scent amen till Prue Derry thought tit hiss sequel toothy heave in moored iffy cult ask owe falling thought Ruth how tin two they'll height, inn haul lit snake head hid dais yes ness.

Womb mend aside they'll are jaw quest shins offal I've cur wreck Tillie end quack lea, knot big horse the Yore lackey gassers, snot big horse their dough vine lea inns spy yard, knot big horse the ape rack toss sum Madge hick kin hairy Ted frames have edge hairy, bats sump plea ends holy big horse the hove cents. This heat hag lance watt mows tomb hen cooed knot sew eth sir chill heights sand Tallis copes.

Their rat gripes withy ass hen shells off up rob limb beef form hen hove Finnish dub eight ting gats smear axed earn ills. The ear this up ream real lists off their ace. Up parent lea ill lodge hick ill, their though Poe's cess sirs offer air ends settle soup purl lodge hick.

Up parent lea wee musical, the yang toothy true with wither ton asset tea witch curries thumb threw aver rhea face off fits sin cess ant, jell lea lick shafting off farm. Up parent lean knob servant tanned ass heaved, this he wit bride end whore rubble ice.

Inn meant who, this aim arse sill lisp Erse pick ass cities hum thymes shoes sits elf—min rack Hogin eye Sid two bee moral hoof fend dun inflame able thin thee gin oral—min off spay shelled Hal lint four they'll lodge hick ills—hard on Nick mince, sin necks. Meant who, summit thymes hove bray inns. Bat thought hisser air, airman, I've vent sure, rue whiz ass Ted alley hint hell agent, ass cons tan Tillie's hound dinge hadj mint, hassle idyll putt Taff buy up ear rinses, ass they've ridge womb man off fort tea ate.

Annie bell lea, Head gear all in po, 1849

Hit worse men knee aye ear rug hoe
Winner king dumb buy this see,
Thought hum aid din there'll hived tomb ewe main hoe,
Buy thin aim off fanny bill lea,
End thus made hen shill hived wit know wither that
Thin tool hove hand bee luffed buy may,
Eye whiz itch aisled end shoe whiz itch aisled,
Inn thus king dumb buy this he;
Bat wheel huffed wither luff thought whiz moor thin luff,
Eye yawned may Hannibal he,
Wither luff thought thaw win gad sir roughs inn haven
Cove ate head end may.
End thus whiz their ease sin thought, lung hag go
Inn thus king dumb buy this he,
Awe wend blue hout huff feck loud, shilling
May beaut awful Ann nibble he;
Sooth hatter rye borne keen some men Kay hum
Mend boar hairy weigh frame he,
Two shatter upon ass sepal cur,
Inn thus king dumb buy this he.
The inn gels, knot Taff sew hap peon hay van,
When ten vying hair end may,
Hess! Thought whiz there he sun (ass sole min no,
Inn thus king dumb buy this he)
Thought though whined Kay mow tough thick loud bine height,
Shilling end culling may Hannibal lea.
Batter luff fit whist wrong herb buy fair thin though luff
Off though sue wear roll door thin wee,
Off Manny fore why sir thin wee
End nigh their thee hain gels sin have van knob off
Gnaw thud deem Huns dow nun door this see,
Kin never diss ever mice hole frame these whole
Off thee beaut awful Ann nibble he;
Four thumb mew in ever be hymns, with hout Bryn gun mid reams
Off thaw beaut awful Ann nibble he
Yawned this Tarzan ever eyes, bat eye fill though Brit ties

Off thee beaut awful Ann nibble he;
Yawned sew, wall thin height hide, isle lied dow win buy this hide
Off may dare lung, may dare lung, mile lie fend maybe ride,
Inner sepal cur their buy this see.

This peck old banned, Cone end oil, 1892

Homes Sid brow tap all lung think Cain, end thus seep laced up on though bid bus hide hymn. Bite heal aid though backs off mat chess sand thus tum puffer can doll. Thin eat earned own they'll amp, penned wee whirl eft tinned ark ness.

Howe shell eye aver fur get thought red fool veg ill? Ike hood knot tear wrasse hound, knot tee van thud raw wing offer bray thinned jet eye new thought mike hump onions hat toe pin night, with inner phew fee tough mien this aims Tate off gnar fuss ten shun inn witch eye whiz mice elf. This shot hers cat tough they'll lea stray offal height, tend wee way Ted din nabs soul Ute dork ness.

Frame hout side Kim Theo Kay shun elk rye off inn height burred, dinned wants sat tower fairy rowan wind hoe wall hung drone cattle Ike wine, witch tolled ass thought thatch eater whiz hat lubber tea. Farrow hay wick hood earth thud heaped hones off though par rush clack, witch bummed doubt aver rick wary her off fan our.

Howl hong this seamed, though squirt hers! 12's truck, end 1 end 2 end 3, ends till wheeze hat way tongues high lent lea four watt haver mite biff all.

Sadden leather whiz thumb home ant airy glee move all height upon thud erection off they've vent till hater, witch van ash tum mead he hat lea, bat whiz acceded buyers straw wings mell off burr nun Goy land he Ted met tall.

Sum wan nun thin hexed rheum addle littered ark lent earn. Eye herd age gent tills hound off move mint, tanned thin knoll whiz high lent wants mower, thaw this mell grue strung her. Four have inn our eyes hat wits training gears.

Thin sadden lean others hound big came Maud able—average gent all, sue things hound, lick thought offers mall Jay toughs team mass cape ping can tin you alley frame Mick cattle. Thee in stint thought wee herd hit, tomes spraying frame though beads, truck ham hatch, chinned dull ash shed few rye us lea withies Cain gnat though bull pool.

"Ewes heat, What's on?" high hell lid. "Ewes seat?"

Bat eyes haw no thin. Hat thumb hoe mint win gnomes truck they'll height tie herd dill oak, leer we sole, bat this sodden gull air flushing inn two may wee rye ice may debt imp passable form heat hoot hell watt tit worse hat witch miff rend latched sews have age lea. Ike hood, how wavers, heath hat huss phase whizzed head leap ale land filed wit whore roar rand low thing.

Ghee hid see Sid twos trike end whisk hazing hop pat though vent till later whin sadden lea their brow wick frame this high lance off thin height thumb host Tory bilk rye two witch eye hove aver list tinned. Hits well dope Lauda rend

Lauda, awe horse shell off paean end fee rand dang her roll Ming gold inn thee wand red filch reek.

This hay thought aweigh dow win inn though fill age, end heave in inn though diss tanned parse sun age, thought crier aced this leapers frame there bids. Sits truck old tour arts.

Eyes two'd gay sing hat tomes, end heat mien till they'll lass tick hoes off fit head eyed aweigh inn two this high lance frame witch hit rows.

"Watt cannot mien?" high gas pad.

"Hit miens thought titties soul lover," roams Ann sword. "End purr hops, softer haul, lit hiss four though bussed. Tay cure pissed hole, land wee well lent her dock tour Roy lots rheum."

Wither grieve fey seal hit they'll amp penned lead thaw weighed own thick carry dirt. Why seas truck cat thatch aim bird whore with hout ten near apply frame with inn.

Thin neat earned thee hand dull land dent herd, eye hat hiss seals, wither cock hid pissed hole lin may and.

Debt whiz ass sing you Lars height witch mate her ice. Sun that able stud add ark lent turn wit though shut her huff foe pin, through wing gob really ant bee muffle height up on this save, thud whore off witch worse edge are.

Bees hide the stable, wan thaw hood inch hairs, hat dock tore grimes bee Roy let cull had dinner lung grade wrasse sing own, ness bear rank hills purr wrote rude hing bin heath, thinned hiss feat throw stun tour head he lest her cash slappers.

A cross suss slap play thee shirts tack withy lung all ash switch weed no tossed you ring thud hay.

Hissed shin whisk hocked up words sand huss sighs wharf hicks dinner dread fool, rid jets tare rat thick horn near off this healing. Rowan diss braw we head up hack Yule ear banned, wit brow gnash spic holes, switches seamed tube Hebe hound tie Tillie rowan diss said. Ass wee interred him aid knee there's hound gnawer mow shun.

"Though banned! This peck hold banned!" wisp eared domes.

Final editor's note …

As everybody knows, there is an infinite number of parallel universes out there. Imagine a vast row of zillions of plates, standing on edge, in a drying rack. Each one is a universe slightly different to the one beside it.

The spaces in between are known as 'skeeters'. If we go down the row of skeeters, we will inevitably come to a number of universes in which the written language is seriously different. The word 'sklyzjc' might, in another universe, be 'fkrzyz' or 'vsztrzy' or 'szyrzbn' and so on.

But before I get a letter from an irate resident of Lodz (pronounced Wodge in Universal Language) complaining that I've just insulted his maternal grandmother, let's end with a brief look at the history of this parallel universe: the post-Armstrong one in which you have, so far, been traveling (struggling? despairing? foaming at the mouth?).

Here's a timeline (added apparently as a post-script to the manuscript) of how things went, over their last few millennia. Turns out that, in some cases, events weren't that different from our own.

THYME LION OFF HIS TOE RICK A VENTS 15,000BC–2095AD

BC

12,000	Furs Timmy grunts frame maize yet two hum Erica rack cross though Bare rings traits
10,000	Cull man nation off they'll lass tie sage
5,000	Brit tin big homes sin aisle hand wen they'll hand burr ridge withy cone tenant's brow kin buy mell tin nice
2,700	Hold king dumb (though perry mad edge) big gun sin he gypped
1,600	Hebe rues are hive inn he gypped
1,250	Is rail light sin vade pal ass stein
753	Found hay shun off row mitt hilly
336	A sassy nation off Fill up off Mass add-on, access shin off All axe an door thug rate
55	Jew lea ass sees her end row manse sin fade Brit tin

AD

4	Berth huff gee suss
570	Berth off mow ham had
711	Sack suss fool more ash shin vase shun of Spay inn lead bite Tar rick
929	Gude kin Gwen says lass off bow he mere dice
1000	Leaf ferric sand as covers Hum Erica
1066	Norm an con quest off Ingle hand dun door Will yum though con cure whore
1094	Hell Sid hakes Vole lance hear
1170	More dare off Sam you well Back hit tin can't her berry Kath heed drill
1189	There rid crews aid toothy wholly lend lunched, wit rich hard though line hart
1290	Axe pulse shun off juice frame mingle hand: hare lip hog rum
1338	Big inning off hand red yours swore, Ingle hand end Fronds
1348	Blacked eth wretch ass your rope
1415	Bottle off a gin core, hen rhea V
1517	Mar ten Loo there nay ills sup hiss nine to fife these seas, reefer may shun big inns
1564	Shakes peer borne, Mike hall Ann jello dice
1588	Deaf feet off Span ash arm adder
1620	Pill grim feathers set till lin Hum Erica
1642	Hout brick off ingle ash sieve ill wore
1649	Axe sick you shun off Char less I. Ingle hand know hick come man well eth
1665	Grate play gun Ingle hand

1666	Grate fie rough Land din. New ton diss cover slaw off gravy tea
1773	Boss tint heap arty
1776	You ass deckle array shin off fin deep pen dance
1777	Sore render off Brit ash harm me hats sari toga
1787	Ham Eric an cons state you shunned rafted
1789	Wash shin tone1st you ass press sad dent. For wrench revel you shins tarts.
1805	Bottle loft rough fall gore
1815	Bottle off water lieu. Knap pole yin fine alley beat tin
1837	Vic Tory ass suck seeds toothy Brit ash thrown
1848	Commune hissed Manny fist toe prod used buy mark sand dangles
1861	US sieve all wore brakes hout. Con fed her ate sucks Hess sat Buller Hun
1876	Bottle off Beg urn, Cast herd off eat head buys who wind yens, hitting ball
1903	Or villain Will burr rite, fur rust can't rolled have year thin hair fly it
1906	Sieve ear hearth quick dust Royce an France hiss go
1909	Hen reef horde 'inn vents' mess prod duck shun withy mad dull teach assay
1912	Hun sin kibble Tit tannic knot Huns ink Hubble aft are hole
1914	Big inning off whirled wore wan
1917	Hum Erica joy yin sin WW1
1918	All lies whin WW1
1919	Dire wrecked fly tack cross settle antic buy All cock end brow in

1928	Wee men hen French eyes din Brit tin, end luck fore word two rue ling though whirled
1929	Ham Eric inns lump panned waltz treat crèche
1938	Host tree Ann next buy jar money, a dull fit lore
1939	Whirled wart who big inns inure rope
1941	Sneak key hat tack con purl arbor badge upper knees
1945	All lies whin WWII. Her rush him ma, Nag a sack eye, axe perry hence thee hat tomb bum, Hun conned dish in all sir ender badge upper knees (soap rise, soap rise!)
1950	Big inning off Core Ian wore
1953	Aver wrist con curd buy Hill hurry end Ten sing
1962	Cue ban miss aisle cry sis rise solved, Check canny dais tans hop two rations
1963	Thaw hole whirled morns thumb herd dour off JFK
1964	They've yet numb wore big inns tug hits seer rhea us
1968	Mar tin loot there kin gas sassy neigh Ted
1969	CARNAL KNEEL HAMSTRUNG forced purse sin two-step own thumb hoon
1974	Press a dent nicks sinner ease signs sunder press your rough imp each mint
1990	Burr lin wool cams Dow in, big inning off thud am ease off come you nizam
1991	Does arts term big inns, wore rug hence tie rack end Sad damn huss Seine
1995	USA wrist whores deep low mat hick reel lay shuns wit via yet numb
1997	Prints Hess die Anna kilt ink hark rash inn Parr hiss
2000	Jaw urge dub yob hush shill lack Ted Press add dent off though USA

2001	All quay Yid dare hat tax awn though whirled raids cent her rand panty gone
2003	Bushed Dick Clare's glow ball 'wore runt error'
2004	Hole limp pick aims rat earn two grease
2095	CARNAL KNEEL HAMSTRUNG IV go speck inn thyme, squash hiss hum moss skeeter, chain jazz though you knee verses winnow wit

978-0-595-49043-1
0-595-49043-3

Lightning Source UK Ltd.
Milton Keynes UK
UKOW041144101212

203439UK00002B/661/P